"I'm Not

Holly said.

"Not helpless, no. Definitely beautiful." He brushed his thumb over the curve of her jaw. "Downright magical."

At that moment Holly did feel helpless. Helpless to deny the excitement, the sheer pleasure of his touch.

Without taking his eyes from hers, Rick lowered his mouth to her lips and kissed her. Softly. Sensually.

Holly leaned into the enveloping warmth of his arms. She saw the flare of hunger in his eyes before closing her own.

Growling husky words of pleasure, Rick deepened the kiss with an ardent fierceness that Holly welcomed.

She shifted against him, almost making him explode.

"Oh..."

The tortured sound of his voice made her open her eyes.

"I think we should—" she began.

"Don't think," he interrupted her, his lips feathering across the pulse beating at the base of her throat. "Just feel."

Dear Reader,

Welcome to May! We're delighted to bring you six wonderful books by some of your favourite authors.

Calhoun is Diana Palmer's first title in her exciting twelve book mini-series, TEXAN LOVERS. For the next year, there will be one Diana Palmer each month, which we're certain you'll want to give pride of place on your bookshelves.

There's another sexy Texas man to be found in the last of Barbara McCauley's HEARTS OF STONE titles, *Texas Pride*. Dylan Grant wants Jessica Stone to accept his offer of help to rebuild her life—but she is determined to go it alone.

Blaine O'Connor is a *Father in the Making* in Marie Ferrarella's heartwarming MAN OF THE MONTH title, and you'll meet another of THE TANNER BROTHERS in Anne McAllister's *Cowboys Don't Stay*. And the month is completed with Andrea Edwards' *Starting Over* and Cathie Linz's *Escapades*—two more sparkling stories not to be missed!

So, until next month, happy reading.

The Editors

Escapades

CATHIE LINZ

*First published in Great Britain 1996
by Silhouette Books, Eton House, 18-24 Paradise Road,
Richmond, Surrey TW9 1SR*

© Cathie Baumgardner 1993

*Silhouette, Silhouette Desire and Colophon are
Trade Marks of Harlequin Enterprises II B.V.*

ISBN 0 373 05804 7

Made and printed in Great Britain

CATHIE LINZ

was in her mid-twenties when she left her career in a university law library to become a full-time writer of contemporary romance fiction. Since then, this popular Chicago author has had numerous books published. She enjoys hearing from readers and has received fan mail from as far away as Nigeria!

An avid world traveller, Cathie often uses humorous mishaps from her own trips as inspiration for her stories. Such was the case with this book, inspired by a recent trip to the Cascade Mountains in Washington State. Even so, Cathie is always glad to get back home to her two cats, her trusty word processor and her hidden cache of cookies!

Other Silhouette Books by Cathie Linz

Silhouette Desire

Change of Heart
A Friend in Need
As Good as Gold
Adam's Way
Smiles
Handyman
Smooth Sailing
Flirting with Trouble
Male Ordered Brides
Midnight Ice
Bridal Blues
A Wife in Time

For Bob Denholm,
an extraordinary bookseller and a very special man,
who made me part of his extended family.
He is missed and will not be forgotten.

Prologue

"**I** don't care if you have to tie her up and gag her! I want you to bring my daughter back."

Rick Dunbar didn't say a word as he took note of the rich office furnishings around him. Clearly Howard Redmond, president of Redmond Imports, was doing very well. And clearly Howard was very upset about his daughter.

Which is where Rick fit in. He was a private investigator. Locator of missing persons. Surveillant of wayward spouses. For the right price.

"You say you want me to bring your daughter back," Rick said. "Back from where?"

"I don't know where she is right now. Last I heard she was up in Alaska. I've written down what I do know." Howard handed Rick an envelope—a thick envelope.

Rick knew better than to think it was filled with money. Guys like Howard Redmond held on to their dollars with both fists tightly closed.

"My daughter has indulged in plenty of escapades," Howard was saying. "I've listed a few of them there. You wouldn't believe the things she's gotten into. Oh, and I've included a check for one thousand dollars," Howard casually added. "You'll get another thousand when you find her and the final three thousand when you bring her back."

Rick had been sitting there listening to Howard Redmond ranting about his daughter for almost an hour now. Howard's story wasn't a new one to Rick. He'd been hired to return reckless debutantes before. As far as Rick was concerned, it was time to cut to the chase—negotiating his fee. "Make it five thousand up front and five when I bring her back and you've got a deal."

Howard frowned and gave Rick a glare that would intimidate most men from twenty paces away.

Rick didn't even blink. At thirty-four, there was little in life that intimidated or impressed him.

"There are other private investigators in Seattle, you know," Howard said.

"None as good as I am," Rick calmly replied.

Howard smiled grudgingly. Rick had come highly recommended by Howard's closest friend—his *only* friend—who'd used Rick on his divorce case. The information Rick had dug up on the man's now ex-wife had saved the day. "You strike a hard bargain, Dunbar. All right. Five thousand up front and five when you bring her in."

"Deal."

Still, Rick could tell as he watched Howard make out an additional check that the old man hated parting with his money.

"If she weren't my only daughter..." Howard reluctantly handed over the check.

Rick handed it right back. "You didn't sign it."

"Oh."

Once the signed check was safely in Rick's inner pocket, he said, "You say your daughter was in Alaska the last you knew?"

Howard's nod reflected his aggravation. "The way she behaves you'd think we were still in the sixties."

Rick's expression hardened. "She's into drugs?"

"No, thank God! Just health food. She's a vegetarian," Howard added in disgust.

Being a steak-and-potato man himself, Rick grimaced.

"You'd think she'd grow up," Howard continued. "Be willing to accept some responsibility. It's not as if Holly is still a teenager. She's twenty-eight. I can't keep running the business by myself forever. I've given her plenty of time to find herself. My patience has run out. Her time is up. I want her back here in Seattle with me."

"I gather she doesn't want to come back willingly," Rick noted dryly.

"She doesn't know what she wants!" Howard maintained. "Holly is a flighty female, if ever I've seen one. Just like her mother, God rest her soul. Don't get me wrong. I loved my wife, but the poor woman couldn't rub two thoughts together. Sweet as could be and gorgeous. Just didn't have a very long attention span. Holly is the same way."

Rick was skeptical about Howard's wanting someone that flighty taking over what appeared to be a very successful import business—but, hey, that was Howard's problem, not his.

Glancing down, Rick concentrated on the first of several typed sheets he held in his hand. Holly Redmond had clearly led an unorthodox life. "How did she get hooked up with a communal fishing cannery?"

"She started it. She's always starting something," Howard muttered.

Rick skimmed through some of the other listings. "Communal flower farm, communal craft school . . . Your daughter seems to have a thing for communal projects. She involved in any kind of religious cult?"

"That's what I'm paying you to find out," Howard countered. "And to bring my daughter back. The sooner the better. God knows what she's gotten herself into by now!"

One

Freedom. Holly Redmond loved it. The freedom to do what she wanted, to say what she wanted, to be whatever she wanted. It was something she'd longed for all her life. She was free now—but only because she'd fought for that right. Fought hard and never looked back. Because some things were worth risking everything for.

Holly had never been one to dwell on the past, so she didn't know why she was suddenly doing so now. It was July, too late to attribute her behavior to spring fever. And the sun was shining, a thrill to anyone who spent much time in this part of Washington state, so she couldn't blame her mood on the weather, either.

So what was she doing inside on such a lovely day? she asked herself while carefully molding the wet piece of clay on the potter's wheel in front of her. The answer was that she was trying to prove something. She'd never been one to resist a challenge, and right now the challenge was learning how to properly throw a pot instead of having it collapse like a limp dishrag. So far, no luck.

Since her hands were wet, Holly had to use her forearm to shove her blond hair out of her eyes. The curly strands were rebelling against the restraint of the hair clasp. Like Holly, her hair also loved its freedom.

There were a million and one things she needed to get done today, including looking over the latest batch of participant response forms. At the moment, however, she needed this stolen half hour to herself. As founder and director of Inner View, Holly was the one everyone else looked to for leadership and a sense of direction. Holly had to grin when she reflected upon the irony of a free spirit like her ending up in an honest-to-goodness position of authority.

Looking back, she could see now that all the projects she'd been involved in before—and there had been plenty of them—had been leading to this one. The work that went on here was very important to Holly. She liked to think she was making a difference in people's lives—improving their self-esteem and self-confidence.

To Holly's way of thinking, she was simply returning the favor that had once been done for her. She knew what it felt like to have her spirit broken, to have her self-confidence crushed.

The memory made her grin disappear. It had been a long time ago; she'd only been eight years old, but Holly had never forgotten. . . .

"Your mother is dead. Nothing we can do about it. Crying won't bring her back, either, so stop sniveling, girl!" her father had ordered her. "A Redmond never snivels. Never cries. Why, that mother of yours spoiled you rotten. Look at you—look at this mess!" With an angry sweep of his hand, he'd sent her paintings and watercolor set—the one Holly's mother had given her—flying.

Even now, Holly could still remember the shaking fury she'd felt at his action, fury that he'd ruined the one thing she had left of her mother's. Holly had already watched in dismay as her father had cleared out all her mother's belongings within an hour of her death. It was as if he couldn't wait to erase all signs of her beloved mother ever having existed. His destruction of her mother's final present to her had been the last straw as far as Holly was concerned.

Holly had flown at him, kicking, crying, screaming in pain. Her father had held her off as if she were nothing more than an obnoxious insect . . . until she'd collapsed, sobbing, at his feet. He'd left her there as he walked away.

Early the next morning Holly was placed on a plane, heading from Sacramento to a boarding school in New England. ''They'll teach you some respect there, girl'' were her father's parting words. ''And you'd better learn it well, if you know what's good for you.''

The boarding school hadn't been good for her. Or *to* her. Withholding affection, approval, acknowledgment, they'd almost broken her. But an art teacher there had saved her, praising her artwork. A little glimmer of light, enough to sow the seeds of self-esteem and let them grow.

In that school and others, countless authority-minded adults had tried to whip her into shape, to mold Holly into the kind of blindly obedient and docile daughter her father wanted. But they had never succeeded. Because of that hidden source of strength inside of Holly, a source that had started with that single glimmer of light.

Holly had come a long way since then. She was light years away from the controlling father who'd held her in his iron-fisted grip until she'd reached the age of eighteen.

Glancing at her waterproof watch—the one with Van Gogh on the face—she realized that if she didn't hurry, she'd be late for the children's finger-painting class she was supposed to be teaching in fifteen minutes.

The class turned out wilder than usual as the ten students tried to put the paint in each other's hair instead of on the paper.

Things then went from bad to worse. Holly barely made it back to her cabin after class when Skye came rushing in. In her early forties, her long black hair slashed with gray and bound in a loose braid, Skye was the original earth mother. Skye had come of age during the sixties and she'd never grown out of that age of Aquarius. She could bake her own bread, weave her own material and blend the best herbal tea Holly had ever tasted. In fact, the only things Skye couldn't do were balance a checkbook, hold down a regular nine-to-five job or vote Republican.

More than a friend, Holly considered Skye to be a member of her extended family—a family Holly had gathered around her here at Inner View.

"You're needed in the main office," Skye told Holly in a rush. "Better hurry." Without waiting for further explanation, Holly immediately turned around and raced off to the building that functioned as Inner View's headquarters and office. There she found her assistant, Charity, frantically stuffing things into a baby carrier.

"What's the matter?" Holly asked.

"It's my baby!" Charity replied. "She's got a high fever and the doctor wants me to bring her in to his office right away. Guido's going to drive me. He's already in the truck with the baby."

"I'll cover for you here, Charity," Holly hastily assured her. "Don't worry. Doc Broncasio knows what he's doing. He'll take good care of Sunshine."

Charity grabbed a diaper bag, mumbling something about an accountant executive named Potter coming by today.

"I'll handle it," Holly stated.

Before handling anything, however, Holly decided she'd better clean off the finger paint still adorning her arms as a result of her earlier run-in with her obstreperous students. And so it went...another quiet day here at Inner View, Holly noted with a rueful grin before heading to the back of the office to clean up.

Rick got out of his car and stretched. It had been a two-hour drive from Seattle to Inner View. He'd verified by phone that Holly Redmond was indeed here before driving up. Not wanting to scare her off, he hadn't asked to speak to her personally, however. With her record, she was obviously the flighty sort, and God knew he didn't want to have to track her down again.

He'd already traced her from Alaska to Arizona and back again, only to find she'd landed here—practically in his backyard. He had quickly packed a light bag and headed up to the mountains. Hopefully he'd be able to wrap up this job sooner than he'd anticipated.

Rick still wasn't sure what kind of place this "Inner View" was supposed to be. The answer he'd gotten over the phone—an Institute for Creative Development—didn't tell him a whole hell of a lot and he certainly hadn't wanted to raise suspicions by asking too many questions. Instead, he'd traced the location from the phone number he had and then he'd opted to drive up here himself and get some firsthand information.

A hand-painted wooden sign strategically placed along the only main road through that area had precluded the need for him to stop in town and ask for specific directions. Another sign, a carved wooden one this time, had led him down a winding gravel road that had ended here at the camp.

To his right, Rick saw a number of log cabins lined up with military precision. Straight ahead of him was a lake.

Beyond that, scenically rising above the forested hills, he recognized the snowy shape of Mount Rainier. To his left were another group of cabins, these placed much more haphazardly than the others he'd seen. The largest and closest of these buildings had another carved wooden sign on it claiming it was the Inner View Center.

Rick was about to move toward the building when a woman in her forties came into view, holding a child of about three by the hand. As they came nearer, the red-headed little girl waved and smiled at him.

"I gotta vagina . . . and you don't," the little girl cheerfully informed Rick in a singsong voice.

Rick almost fell over in shock.

The woman with the little girl just shrugged and smiled. "She's at an age where she's exploring her sexual identity," she said as if by way of explanation.

Not wanting to stick around to see if the kid was going to discuss *his* anatomy as well as her own, Rick hightailed it into the building as if the hounds of hell were at his heels.

The insistent sound of a ringing phone greeted him even before he entered the building. The bang of the screen door slamming behind Rick heralded his hurried arrival. He looked around but there was no one in sight.

From somewhere in the back, a woman shouted, "Either answer that phone or shoot it!"

Two

Rick chose to answer the phone rather than shoot it. Picking up the receiver ended its electronic shrieking. Rick had barely said, "Hello," when a curt male voice on the other end of the phone line briskly said, "This is Potter. I have to make an emergency business trip down to San Francisco, so I'm canceling my reservation. I won't be coming today." Without waiting for a reply, the caller hung up.

Reservation? What kind of commune was this? Rick wondered with a frown. A *yuppie* commune?

Before he could consider the matter further, however, a woman strolled into view. And not just any woman. Holly Redmond. Rick recognized her from the photo Howard had shown him, but it hadn't given him a hint of her sex appeal. She had a sassy walk and a curvaceous body. Her bright orange jeans fit her like a glove.

Rick's eyes moved upward in silent appreciation. He liked her hair. The blond curls were piled on top of her head in a rather haphazard way that he found very appealing. Unlike the blondes he knew, her eyes were brown, not blue. A rich, velvety brown that made him think of the brown velvet bedspread on his bed, and how she'd look sprawled out on it.

So this was the woman who had a thing for escapades. Rick found himself wondering what else Holly had a thing for.

She wore no rings, but she was wearing a strange necklace made of brightly painted wooden fish. Her earrings, on the other hand, were silver—large dangling fish holding fishing poles with... Rick squinted. The *fish* were holding the fishing poles with a man suspended from the end.

He wondered if she was making some kind of statement here, even as he noticed the way the silver earrings jauntily swung against Holly's slim neck when she leaned toward him.

"Ah, you must be Mr. Potter," Holly said, offering him her hand.

Rick saw his chance and grabbed it... along with her hand. "That's right. I'm Mr. Potter," he said, wrapping his fingers around hers. Her hand looked delicate and dainty, swallowed up as it was in his clasp. Her skin was soft and warm and... slippery?

"Sorry," Holly murmured, tugging her fingers free. "I just put on hand cream. Now you'll smell like honey and almond until you wash your hands. Anyway, welcome to Inner View. I'm Holly Redmond and we've been expecting you. I didn't mean to yell that way... about answering the phone, I mean." Holly looked at the now silent phone. "I guess the caller must have hung up. No matter, they'll call back again. We're usually a little more on top of things, but it's just been one of those days. You know how it goes...."

She was babbling, and she knew it wasn't like her. But then this man wasn't like any guest she'd ever seen. Not here at Inner View.

The phone may have stopped ringing, but Holly's senses were definitely still humming. This never happened to her. She'd met plenty of men in the course of her travels, had shaken hundreds of hands. The only time she'd come close to feeling this way was when she'd gotten an electrical shock from a faulty toaster!

Judging from his appearance, there was nothing faulty about this man, although he was far removed from the button-down analytical adults who usually checked in here. He didn't look like one of the kid's dads, either.

He looked . . . rough and somewhat dangerous. Not the kind of danger that made her worry about protecting the cash drawer. This was the kind of sensual danger that made her worry about protecting her virtue. Because this man had too much raw male magnetism for his own good—let alone hers.

In his early thirties, with dark hair and cynical eyes, he was wearing a denim shirt and jeans. He radiated sex appeal—the glow-in-the-dark kind.

"You know, you don't really look like an accountant," Holly noted.

"Neither do you," Rick replied, wondering where that off-the-wall comment had come from.

"Yes, but I'm *not* an accountant. You *are.*"

This was news to Rick. So . . . Potter was an accountant, huh? Granted his own arithmetic was limited to subtracting his debts from his income, but that didn't bother Rick. He knew that the best defence was a good offence. So he said, "What makes you think I don't look like an accountant?"

"You look too . . ." What could she say? That he looked too sexy? Too dangerous? Too confident? "You look too relaxed," she improvised.

"Relaxed?" Rick repeated.

"Never mind. Anyway, we've got everything ready for you. The accommodations aren't fancy, but the beds are comfortable and our instructors can't be beat. You've already missed the orientation meeting, unfortunately, but if you've read the information we sent you as part of your registration packet you'll have a pretty fair idea of what we do here."

"I didn't have time to read my registration packet, so why don't you run the basics by me right now."

"Ah, another bottom-liner," Holly noted.

"What?"

"You just want the bottom line, which makes you a bottom-liner. It's a problem a lot of our guests have when they first arrive. We're going to change that. Change the way you think."

"What is this?" Rick asked suspiciously. "Some kind of brainwashing center?"

"Not at all."

"So what's the deal? Are you trying to sell me something or convert me to some religion?"

"Neither. We're simply going to open you up to new kinds of problem-solving techniques. New approaches in managing problems and people."

Management seminars? Rick hadn't been living in the Dark Ages. He knew middle managers, the guys in the suits, were being forced to attend management seminars these days. He just didn't know how that fit in with Inner View. This camp, out in the middle of no place, didn't look like the normal site for business seminars.

But then, as Rick well knew from researching her background, Holly was never involved with anything that was normal. "So you give management seminars here?" he asked.

"Creativity seminars," Holly corrected him. "You should have read your brochure." She paused, intending to use his first name in her chastisement, only to realize she didn't know it.

"I don't seem to have your first name written down here." *Or if we do, I can't find it,* Holly silently tacked on. Given Charity's rushed departure, the paperwork on this particular guest was nowhere to be found. "We're very informal here, so we can't keep calling you Mr. Potter. What is your first name?"

"You can call me Rick."

"Rick." She now had a name to go along with the sexy man who was presently eyeing her shirtfront with more than polite interest! She frowned at him. "You should have read your brochure, Rick."

"And miss this personal presentation?" he murmured with devilish softness. "No way."

Holly was no shrinking violet, but his provocative gaze made her feel self-conscious, a rare occurrence for her. Equally uncommon was the way her toes were curling and her pulse racing as if she'd just finished an aerobic workout.

Holly decided to confront him directly. "What are you looking at?" she demanded.

"You've got paint on your T-shirt."

"I do? Where?" Looking down, she didn't see anything untoward. All she saw was the rapid rise and fall of her breasts. Was *he* noticing? Holly hoped not. "I don't see any paint."

"Want me to point it out?" he offered suggestively.

"Forget it. Just tell me where it is."

"The paint is all over."

"You mean these?" She tugged her T-shirt away from her body, intending to show him the pattern on the shirt without drawing attention to the curves under it. "These are handprints. It's a handmade T-shirt. One of our guests made it for me."

"Very impressive," Rick said, the tone of his voice suggesting that he was referring to what was *under* the T-shirt, not the design on top of it.

He finally looked up into her eyes. "So that's all you guys do here?" Rick said. "Sit around and be creative? Doing what . . . painting flowers and stuff?"

His patronizing tone of voice angered Holly. So had his blatant appraisal of her, as well as her own unexpected physical reaction to him. "No, that's not all we do here," she retorted.

"Good." If Rick was going to be stuck out here for a few days, figuring out how to deliver the goods to Redmond senior, he certainly didn't want to be stuck doing any sissy arts-and-crafts stuff.

"As well as painting, we also offer sculpting, weaving and pottery, to name just a few," she deliberately added.

"Great." Rick sounded as undelighted as he felt.

"Don't worry, Rick," she advised him mockingly. "We'll have you viewing the world in a new way before you know it."

And before *you* know it, I'll have you back in Seattle, Rick thought to himself. Safely returned to her wealthy papa. Now it was just a matter of figuring out how.

Rick wasn't worried about having no predesigned plan in mind. He preferred relying on his gut instincts. And his gut instincts told him that this could turn out to be a very interesting case. At least he wouldn't be bored, not with an unpredictable, sexy woman like Holly around.

Yes, Rick thought to himself. I think I'm gonna like this particular job. A lot.

With that thought in mind, Rick gladly followed Holly outside and across the graveled area to the orderly row of cabins. He left enough of a distance between them that he was able to enjoy the view—not of the surrounding scenery but of the delicious curve of her bottom encased in those brilliant orange jeans. She really did have an incredibly sexy walk. He'd noticed that before but it definitely deserved further contemplation…and appreciation. After all, a sexy walk was an art form all its own. Poetry in motion.

It was a shame she was a client's daughter and therefore off limits, Rick noted with regret.

"Here we are," she stated cheerfully, holding open a cabin door for him.

"Why are there four beds in here?" Rick asked suspiciously.

"Because each cabin has four guests staying there," Holly replied. "The bathroom, which has a shower, is here on the left. Your bed is the one in the corner," she added.

While he appreciated the sway of her fanny as she sashayed in front of him, Rick didn't appreciate the way she seemed to take pleasure in telling him the location of his bed. She sounded like a teacher sending a naughty kid to go sit in the hot seat. And while Rick readily admitted to being naughty, and she was certainly making him hot, he was no kid. Hell, he was a good six years older than she was.

"And what do *you* do here?" Rick asked her. "Aside from showing guests their beds, I mean."

Holly shot him a look over her shoulder. Her brown eyes were so revealing that Rick could actually see the expressions come and go—reminding him of those Christmas tree floodlights that turned an aluminum tree red, and then green, and then yellow. He hadn't seen one of those lighted trees since he was eight. It had also been a long time since he'd seen anyone display their emotions so readily.

He could read her like a book. First he'd seen anger, then the doubt, then he could actually see her thinking, and then a flash of humor. In fact, she was so easy to read that Rick wondered if this wasn't just an act of hers, a way of making others think she was vulnerable when she wasn't.

Most likely the reason she showed so many emotions so quickly was because she didn't feel any of them deeply, he cynically decided. No doubt she was as shallow as the other debutantes he'd dealt with.

"When I'm not showing guests their beds, I run Inner View," Holly belatedly answered his earlier question.

"What do you mean you run it?"

"I'm the director here," she stated.

This flighty woman in charge? Rick was stunned. God forbid. If that was the case, the place would fold in a week. No way it could be successful. He'd have to check that out, now that he knew more about what an Institute for Creative Development was. "These rooms have phones?" he asked.

"No. We have a pay phone near the office for the guests to use."

"No phones?" Rick noted in disbelief. How the hell was he supposed to use the modem on his notebook computer without a phone? That computer was his link, not only to his office but to the resources he needed to get more information on Holly's latest little project here. "Listen, there's work I brought along that has to be done...."

"Participants were warned about the phones in their packet of information. The one you obviously didn't read, Rick."

"What about the phone in the office?"

"It's for staff members' use only."

There were ways of getting around that, and Rick intended to find one. Given their laid-back attitude around here, he doubted these folks even locked the office at night. It shouldn't be too difficult for him to make a little midnight raid of their phone lines, as well as getting some more info on this Potter guy he was impersonating.

That decided, Rick casually inquired, "So, Holly, how long have you been in charge here?"

"Since I thought of the idea of combining business creativity seminars with children's creativity seminars at one center."

"Kids? You didn't say anything about kids before." Rick was appalled. He imagined legions of them . . . all using anatomically correct language!

"Why, Rick, you sound almost panic-stricken at the idea," Holly noted.

"Yeah, I'm just tremblin' in my boots," he retorted sarcastically.

"There's no need to get defensive about it," she told him. "Am I correct in assuming you don't have any children of your own?"

"That's right. I'm not married, either," Rick added.

"I didn't ask," she pointed out.

"No, but you were going to."

She neither denied nor confirmed his assertion. Instead she changed the subject. "Dinner is in half an hour, Rick. The dining hall is the big long building behind the main office. We serve family style and we have vegetarian meals—"

"You don't serve meat?" Rick's irritation was increasing. First no phones and now this?

"We do serve meat to those who must have it."

"Thank God." Rick heaved a sigh of relief. Old man Redmond wasn't paying him enough to be stuck in some artsy-craftsy camp for a week—without phones *and* without meat!

"Not red meat, of course," Holly continued, shattering Rick's visions of a thick, juicy steak. "We serve chicken and fish. We're proud of the healthy menu we provide here. It conforms to the American Heart Association guidelines."

Since Rick was rumored not to even *have* a heart, he'd never worried about that particular organ. Hell, he'd already given up cigarettes to save his lungs. He had to draw the line somewhere. Let other people graze on dandelion greens. He preferred red meat, medium rare. Clearly he'd have to supplement his meals with some side trips into town. "I don't suppose you've got a TV in this place, either?"

"Why would anyone want to stare at a television screen when you're surrounded by all this natural beauty?"

"Because the Mets are playing the Giants tonight." At her blank look, Rick added, "You know, baseball. You have heard of baseball, right?"

"Certainly," Holly replied. "It's that game where men stand on little white things and try and hit a ball with a bat. More often than not, they miss."

"Baseball is this country's national pastime."

"I know. Sad, isn't it?" As he sputtered for an answer, she blithely went on. "Look, I'd love to stay here and chat, but I've got work to do. As I said before, you've already missed the orientation session but you'll get to meet your roommates, as well as the other instructors, at dinner."

Other instructors, he silently repeated. Meaning *she* was one of the instructors? "You actually teach here, as well as running the place?"

"And I show guests their beds—don't leave out that part," she mockingly replied. "Yes, I teach. Do you have a problem with that?"

"No, no problem."

"Then why the disbelief?"

"What disbelief?"

"Your disbelief at the idea of me being a teacher."

So she'd picked up on that, had she? Rick silently vowed that he'd have to be more careful in the future. It really wasn't like him to be careless.

Holly was a cute distraction, but the bottom line was that he was the predator and she was his prey. His job was to catch her, return her to her doting daddy and pick up the rest of his cash. Clean and simple.

Rick reminded himself of the five thousand dollars he'd receive once he'd completed this case. For that kind of money, he could put up with a few inconveniences. He could forgo watching a few ball games and make do with listening to them on his portable radio.

As for sharing a room . . . he hadn't done that since he'd been in the navy. He hadn't liked it then and he still felt the same way about it now. Even the evenings he'd spent in a lovely lady's bedroom had been just that—*evenings*. Not entire nights. Rick had always left afterward and gone home to his own place. Those were the rules. The women involved knew that going in. They had valued their independence as much as he valued his.

Holly stood there, impatiently tapping her foot. "You still haven't answered my question, Rick."

"Sorry," he noted absently. "I was thinking about something else. What was your question again?"

"Forget it," she said, still irked at his reaction to her being an instructor. "I'll leave you alone with your thoughts of balance sheets and numbers."

Rick frowned. Balance sheets and numbers? Realization dawned. Oh, right. He was supposed to be an accountant. Hell, for a supposedly simple case, things were certainly getting complicated here. Time to haul out the old charm and simplify things a bit.

Rick had been told he could be charming when the occasion warranted it. Actually the comment had been that he could be "a charming bastard" when he wanted to be. Rick figured a little charm might just be the ticket where Holly was concerned.

"I'm glad you're an instructor here. I'll look forward to your class. I'm sure you're very good at what you do," he added softly.

"I liked you better when you were being offensive," Holly bluntly informed him. "At least then you were telling the truth. There's nothing I hate more than being lied to."

So much for charm doing the trick, Rick thought to himself. "Everybody lies, in one way or another."

"I don't."

"Right. And I'll bet you don't drink or swear, either."

"I wouldn't say that. I can swear in six languages, including Cantonese."

"An admirable skill, I'm sure."

"It's come in handy on one or two occasions," she replied with a secretive smile.

"And what occasions were those?" he asked.

"Private ones," she said succinctly. "See you at dinner, Rick."

As Holly sailed out of the cabin, Rick silently tallied up the score: fancy lady, one; private investigator, zero. But it was only the first inning, Rick noted confidently. Plenty of time left in the ball game yet.

Three

***

"**T**hat man definitely needs some educating!" Holly muttered under her breath as she marched back to the main office. "Talk about a chauvinist. He acted like I shouldn't even be teaching. As if I weren't qualified. Hah! I'll bet there are plenty of things I could teach him..."

She trailed off, smiling reflectively at the prospect. He'd be a challenge, that was certain. But then she relished tackling challenges and beating the odds. That being the case, Holly was extremely tempted to take on the task of "enlightening" Rick and teaching him the errors of his macho ways.

He really was a...scoundrel. That's the word that came to mind. There was a certain edge to his smile, a mischievous naughtiness that said he had a wicked sense of humor.

That was a shame, Holly ruefully decided. Rick would have been easier to dislike if he hadn't had a sense of humor. It had always been her downfall.

As Holly prepared to lock up the office for the evening, she reflected back on the other men in her life who had caught her attention and awakened her affection.

There had been surprisingly few. Given her nomadic and somewhat unconventional life-style, Holly realized that those who didn't know her well expected her to be far more experienced than she actually was. The truth was, there had only been two serious romantic relationships in her past.

The first had happened while she was in college and had quickly flared out once she discovered the guy only saw her as an easy meal ticket. The second relationship had lasted much longer. She'd thought that Tim had shared her goals in life. Instead he'd tried to change her, to box her in and make her conform to *his* ideas of who and what she should be.

They'd broken up two years ago over Holly's decision to start Inner View. Tim had told her she should invest all her money in him and their future together. He'd given her an ultimatum. In the end, Holly had chosen her freedom...with regret over what could have been, if Tim had been the man she'd thought he was.

Men. Holly shook her head. *They always wanted things their own way.* Rick was another prime example of that infuriating male trait. She'd seen the surprise in his dark blue eyes when she'd bluntly told him she preferred it when he was being offensive since at least then he'd been telling the truth. He'd clearly expected her to fall for his charm the second he'd turned it on. Not her. She wanted more than empty charm and empty promises.

Hopefully Rick would learn a thing or two while he was here at Inner View. If not, she just might have to teach him a thing or two herself....

Rick spent what little time he had left before dinner unpacking the bag he'd thrown into the car to bring with him up to the mountains. It contained the essentials: his shaving kit, a few packages of clean underwear and socks, a handful of T-shirts, two pairs of jeans, a pair of khaki slacks and three clean shirts still in their original wrappers. He unceremoniously tossed everything into the three drawers of the oak cabinet that sat beside his narrow twin bed.

Despite his abbreviated unpacking, Rick was still one of the last to enter the dining hall. It was a fancy name for a plain building. There were two doors, one at either end. Rick always made a point of locating the exits first thing, an old habit that had saved his hide on more than one occasion.

He quickly scouted out the building: cement floor, screened windows all around the outer walls and long tables with red checkered tablecloths. The place was crowded—few of the red plastic chairs were empty. Unfortunately the first person Rick spotted in the sea of faces was the redheaded little girl with the big mouth and anatomically correct vocabulary.

Turning on his heel, Rick immediately headed in the other direction. He'd heard enough from that kid to last a lifetime and had no desire for a repeat performance.

"There's room at our table if you'd like to join us," a woman called out to him. It wasn't Holly's voice, but since she *was* seated at that table, he accepted the invitation.

"Thanks. My name's Rick Potter. And you are . . . ?"

"Sharon Thompson. I'm one of the instructors here. We missed you at the orientation session."

"Couldn't be helped," Rick said with his best smile.

Unlike Holly, Sharon responded to his charm the way a woman was supposed to. That reassured him. Not that he thought he was losing any of his skills, but a few ego strokes never hurt.

Sharon Thompson looked to be in her early fifties. She was dressed in a more conservative manner than Holly, but then, that wasn't hard to do. She had dark hair, cut stylishly short, and she held herself with the confidence of a woman used to being in charge. Rick wondered why *she* wasn't running Inner View instead of Holly.

Throughout the meal, Rick subtly pumped Sharon for information both about the camp and about Holly herself. Since Holly was sitting far enough down the table that she couldn't overhear their conversation, Rick was free to pursue his line of questioning without Holly's knowledge or possible objections.

"So, you used to be a vice president of marketing?" he asked Sharon.

"That's right. When I was coming up in the ranks there weren't many female executives. There are still proportionally few, but back then we were talking *pitifully* few."

"How did you end up here?" Rick asked her.

"Life in the fast track wasn't all it's cracked up to be. I wasn't happy with my life, so I reevaluated my priorities. A wise friend of mine told me something that made sense. She said, 'You know, no one on their deathbed says, Gee I wish I'd spent more time at the office.' That friend was Holly."

"How did you two meet?"

"She was picketing my employer's company because of their treatment of animals. It was a bioresearch company. The head of public relations had just quit, so it was up to me to do some quick damage control before the bad press adversely affected our marketing strategies. I went outside and talked to her. Listened to her complaints, presented them to the board. They didn't pay any attention, of course. But Holly made me think about what I was doing, the kind of company I was working for. I resigned a month later, having accepted a position at a small computer firm owned by another friend of Holly's."

"You quit a good-paying job in a major corporation to go work in some guy's computer company?"

"The 'guy's computer company,' as you put it, is now the third largest supplier of notebook computers in the country. You've probably heard of them." She mentioned the name and it was the maker of the notebook computer Rick owned.

"Holly knows the owner?"

"She's one of the major stockholders. She invested all the money she had when the owner was just starting out. Suffice it to say she's gotten an excellent rate of return on her initial investment."

From checking Holly's credit rating, Rick knew she was financially secure in her own right. He'd assumed she'd gotten the bulk of her nest egg from her doting daddy. A miscalculation on his part. Hopefully, the only one.

"Do you still work for the computer company?"

"I'm on a leave of absence to develop the business seminars here."

"So you're in charge of the business seminars?"

"We don't think in linear terms like that."

"Holly told me she ran the place."

Sharon eyed him with thoughtful speculation. "You must have irritated Holly for her to say that."

"It's not true, then?"

"Sure it's true. But she doesn't make a big deal out of it. What did you say to her?"

"I didn't say anything," Rick denied. "What makes you think I did?"

"Because it takes a lot to irritate Holly. She's normally pretty mellow."

After a hearty meal of oven-roasted chicken, salad and corn on the cob, Rick was feeling a bit more mellow himself. He'd picked up some valuable information from Sharon about Holly, information he planned on using in his quest to get her back to her father. Money wouldn't be a motivating factor for Holly, but her emotions might well be. It sounded to him like she was a sucker for a sob story.

He had yet to speak to Holly herself, however. He'd attempted to make eye contact with her a few times, but she seemed determined to ignore him. She was up and out of her chair before he'd even finished his meal.

"It's hard for Holly to sit still for very long," Sharon said, having noticed Rick's interest.

"You can say that again," Rick murmured, recalling how many different states Holly had resided in over the past few years.

"She's a very special woman," Sharon declared.

For *special,* Rick substituted *different*—as in strange and unusual.

"She has a lot of friends here," Sharon added. "We're like a family at Inner View, and Holly is the glue that keeps us all together. Take Skye, for example. She's known Holly the longest. I believe they attended the same college at one time."

Someone who knew Holly that well could provide him with some valuable insights into which buttons he'd need to push to get Holly to go back to her father. "Which one is Skye?" Rick asked.

"Skye is the woman at the front table over there. She has her hair in a long braid. Skye's husband, Whit, is our cook. Skye teaches weaving. She has five children, two of which are grown up and living in Seattle now. Her youngest is sitting next to her."

"The redhead?"

"That's right."

So Skye was the hippie-type mom to the kid with the big mouth. Which meant he'd have to talk to her when the kid wasn't around. He was also interested to note that she had to be ten or fifteen years older than Holly, who, as far as he could see, was the youngest of the so-called family here at

Inner View. "How many instructors work here?" Rick asked Sharon.

"Five, although we frequently have folks dropping by to assist from time to time. Aside from myself, there are Skye and Holly. And of course there are Guido and Byron. Have you met them yet?"

"No." Names like that, Rick was sure he'd remember.

Guido proved to be as memorable as his name. Rick had a hard time reconciling the fact that this giant hulk of a man created the delicate floral watercolors that Sharon raved about. Guido looked like he would have been right at home in the World Wrestling League. His bald head shone, as did the small gold-hoop earring in his left ear.

"You don't look like an accountant to me," Guido growled at Rick.

"So? You don't look like a watercolor painter to me. What of it?" Rick countered, unfazed.

"I was sitting at the table behind you and I overheard you asking a lot of questions about Holly," Guido continued. His voice reminded Rick of a company commander he had in the navy. It was a voice accustomed to barking rather than speaking. "There any reason for that?"

"She's a beautiful woman," Rick replied.

"Yeah, she is. Just don't go getting any ideas. 'Cause I find out you've hurt her and I'll be very upset. *Capice?*"

"Are you two...close?" Rick asked.

Rick had to give the guy credit—Guido had the menacing glare down pat. Since Rick was an expert at the same glare himself, he liked to think he was something of a connoisseur in the field.

"She's like a daughter to me. You wanna make something of that?"

Having just detected the redheaded kid barreling toward him, Rick briskly replied, "Not at the moment. Later maybe."

Rick attempted to make himself inconspicuous in the crowd, but the kid was like a damn homing device. She didn't give up. Within a few minutes, she had spotted him again and was pointing in his direction. He could just imagine the words that would be coming next, all of them anatomically correct.

Time to blow this pop stand, Rick decided. Turning to head out the exit a few feet away, Rick reached the door the same time as a young man in a wheelchair.

"Age before beauty," the man said with a mocking grin, holding the door open for Rick.

It hadn't really registered before, but Rick now realized that the entrance had a ramp running up to the door.

Following Rick outside, the man added, "Hey, where's the fire?" but Rick was already out of hearing range.

Rick had just rounded the front of the building when he rammed into...Holly.

He knew who it was the second his hands touched her bare arms. She was soft and silky and as vulnerable as a baby bird in his arms. His predatory instincts rose to the fore. He'd captured his prey. He had her trapped against him.

Then she looked up at him and suddenly *he* was the one trapped. Trapped in the warmth of her big brown eyes. Captured by the curve of her mouth. For one brief moment the lines between predator and prey were blurred.

Her body was pressed close to his. She was the perfect height for him. Not so short that he'd get a crick in his neck from bending down to kiss her. And not too tall.

"What's your hurry?" Holly inquired, not the least bit pleased with the breathlessness of her voice. "Someone chasing you?" she added teasingly.

To her surprise, she saw Rick actually look over his shoulder. His expression was a fascinating combination of aggravation and that macho panic that only the male of the species could portray. Holly was dying of curiosity to see what had caused a tough guy like Rick to look like that. Shifting to take a look for herself, she saw Asia standing twenty feet away, waving and grinning. It didn't take Holly long to put two and two together. Skye had mentioned something earlier about Asia's comment in front of the new arrival.

"Do you have something against children?" Holly inquired, belatedly stepping away from Rick.

"Not when they keep their mouths shut," he muttered, relieved to see the good-natured guy in the wheelchair distract the redheaded little girl and lead her in the opposite direction.

"Meaning children should be seen and not heard?"

"That's right," Rick agreed.

"That's archaic," she said.

Rick shrugged. "So I'm archaic."

"I had noticed that."

"I don't have time for kids."

Holly was no longer amused. "I've heard that before. I've dealt with the children that adults like you don't have time for! I've seen the damage done to them. The ruined self-esteem. Young people drinking or taking drugs in a futile effort to feel good about themselves. Low self-esteem is a factor in everything from adolescent suicide to teenage promiscuity and pregancies. We're robbing kids of a decent chance in life by being too busy to nurture them, to make them feel they're important. It's a crime!"

"Whoa." Rick held up both hands as if attempting to hold off a stampede of wild horses. "Slow down. Where did all that come from?"

"I was just stating my opinion. It's something I feel strongly about."

"I got that impression," he said dryly. Holly obviously felt passionately about this, which got him to wondering what else she felt passionately about. Wondering what else would make her eyes light up and her cheeks flush with color.

Noticing Rick's speculative regard, Holly sighed and then smiled a bit sheepishly. "Byron tells me I get too worked up about things. I saw you two talking earlier." At Rick's blank expression, she added, "Outside the dining hall."

"Oh, you mean the guy in the wheelchair. We never got around to introductions." Rick noticed Holly's frown but didn't know which part of his comment caused it—the fact that he'd skipped an introduction or that he'd referred to the wheelchair.

Not that it mattered. Rick wasn't about to change himself to please anyone else. People could either like him or not, it made no difference to him. But they damn well better not try and change him. He was who he was and he made no apologies for it.

"You know, you could certainly use some sensitivity training," Holly informed him.

"Yeah, I've been told that," Rick replied. Actually he'd been told he had the sensitivity of an iguana. But then, women said strange things when they felt they were being jilted.

"You don't sound very sorry about it," Holly noted.

"Probably because I'm *not* sorry. I don't want my consciousness raised or whatever the current psychobabble term of the month is."

"You prefer analytical facts to psychobabble, as you put it?"

"That's right."

"Which is no doubt why you went into mathematics and accounting, right? Because it fulfills your need to categorize and analyze your world."

"Right again." Actually, as a private investigator, Rick's line of work *did* require that he analyze facts.

"I'm glad it makes you happy," she said simply.

Her response surprised him. Here he was, all ready for an argument . . . and she blindsided him with a smiling benediction.

"You *are* happy, aren't you?" Holly tacked on.

Aha! Rick smiled. Here it was. She was swooping in for the kill. This was behavior he could understand. Behavior he could relate to. It was part of the hunting ritual for the prey to try and distract the predator.

"Sure, I'm happy," he replied. He'd be even happier once he had her back in Seattle with her doting dad and he had that final five-thousand-dollar payment in his hands.

"Good. I'm glad you're happy here." She patted his arm. "You see, I told you you'd settle in."

"Hey, wait a second! I never said I was happy *here* . . ."

"Too late to renege now, Rick. See you in the morning." With an impudent wave of her hand, she was gone.

As Rick lay in his hard twin bed later that night, he thought morning would never come. He'd briefly met his other three roommates. He had nothing in common with any of them. Two were engineers of some sort and the third was a middle-management type. He suspected it was the middle-management type who'd been snoring like a buzz saw earlier and was now quiet.

Actually, Rick would even have preferred the snoring to the eerie silence he was hearing now. He couldn't sleep, it was so quiet. He'd tried turning on his portable cassette radio, but the battery had gone dead. He couldn't even get any static on the damn thing.

Instead, every so often, he kept hearing these strange noises. Outside in the darkness. The silence the rest of the time was deafening. It magnified every little noise.

Rick wasn't a man who liked being out of his element. And he felt out of his element now. He had nothing against wilderness, he just didn't have much time or use for it. Street smart, that's what he was. Not one of those yuppie, outdoorsy types with a passion for fresh air. Give him diesel fumes, sirens, city crime, even that obnoxious beeping noise that the garbage trucks made when they backed up. Anything but this god-awful silence interrupted by those occasional weird shuffling noises.

He'd lived in Seattle most of his life, yet he didn't know if there were bears in the forests of Washington state. It wasn't information he'd ever needed before. The shuffling noise came closer to his screened window. Nah, Rick was sure it wasn't a bear. Bears made more noise. It was probably only a raccoon or something. Right?

The shuffling went away, and now he could actually hear the trees swishing in the wind. That did it! It was too much. In his opinion, trees were like kids—meant to be seen, not heard.

Hell, he wasn't going to stay there, kept awake by a stupid bunch of trees! Muttering under his breath, partially for the relief of hearing a human voice even if it was his own, Rick tossed off the covers and grabbed for his jeans, yanking them up over his briefs. There was just enough of a chill in the air to make him tug on a sweatshirt, as well.

He had to get out of here. Maybe if he took a walk and cleared his head, he could get some sleep. But first he should let Moneybags Redmond know that he'd found his flighty daughter, Holly. For that, Rick needed a phone, preferably not the one out in the open.

Rick would have had no trouble with the sorry excuse for a lock at the main office, had someone locked it. As it was, the door was unlocked. Keeping one eye aimed outside, Rick quickly located the phone and pulled a skinny, battered notebook out of his back pocket. Reading off Redmond's number, he placed the call.

Howard Redmond was not pleased to be awakened just after midnight. "Who is it?" the older man barked, not even bothering with a greeting.

"It's Rick Dunbar. I've found your daughter."

"When are you bringing her home?" was the next barked question.

"I'm working on that now. I'll keep you posted."

"Where is she?"

Rick could just imagine the old man coming up here and attempting to recover Holly himself, thereby cutting Rick out of his final payment. "She's here in the Northwest."

"Care to be more specific than that?" Howard sarcastically inquired.

"No."

"She know who you are or why you're there?"

"No."

"Good. I hear tell you've got a way with the ladies, Dunbar. I want you to use those skills. Sweet-talk her into coming home. You know what I mean. Compliment her, charm her. I'll give you ten days. No longer. I'm not particular about the details. Do whatever you have to do to get her back here as quickly as possible."

"What's the big rush?" Rick demanded.

"I told you. I've lost patience. I'm not getting any younger. Besides, there are business reasons why it would be to my advantage to have the next generation of Redmond Imports here in the very near future."

"Even if the next generation is a woman who has a history of escapades?"

"Even then. Besides, she's been flaunting my authority long enough. I won't put up with it any longer."

"She is over twenty-one."

"Look, I don't have to justify my reasons to you, Dunbar. I hired you to do a job and if you're having second thoughts about it, just say so."

"No second thoughts."

"Good. Then stop worrying about my motives and start worrying how you're going to get my daughter back here. She's just a flighty girl. Surely she can't give you too much trouble."

"Nothing I can't handle."

"Good. Handle her, charm her, do whatever it takes. Understand? Just do it." Howard didn't even wait for an answer before hanging up.

Just do it. Right. Nice guy, giving me carte blanche with his only daughter. The real paternal type.

Not that Rick cared what type of old man Redmond was, as long as he got his money. The only requirement he had for his clients was that they paid him on time and in full. That kept things clean and simple, just the way he liked them.

Holly couldn't sleep. She was sitting out on her front porch, holding a mug filled with Skye's special mixture of peppermint-and-chamomile tea, a blend that usually made her feel relaxed and drowsy. Tonight it wasn't working.

Skye would no doubt attribute Holly's restless behavior to the full moon, but Holly placed the blame firmly on Rick's doorstep. *He* was the reason she couldn't sleep tonight. The memory of his body pressed to hers when they'd collided refused to go away. She'd already tried her yoga meditation routine to no avail. And now Skye's surefire tea wasn't working, either. Not a good sign.

As Holly sat there, slowly rocking in her somewhat dilapidated pine rocking chair, she tried to figure out what it was about the man that disturbed her so much. She'd met better-looking men, although none as charismatic. She'd met more aggravating men, but none as challenging. And as far as sex appeal went...no, Rick definitely had to take top honors in that field!

It wasn't a sex appeal based on biceps or good looks. It was something more elusive—something to do with power and confidence—all wrapped up in the way he walked and the way he made her feel, and expressed by the devilish gleam in his eyes, as well as the cynical edge to his smile.

There was also no denying that something strange happened whenever he touched her. From the moment of their first handshake, she'd felt something else at work here. Something you couldn't easily put a label to. Black magic. Attraction. Call it what you would, Holly didn't welcome its presence in her life. Not one bit. Especially with a man like Rick.

He was too...everything. Too sure of himself. Too chauvinistic. Too brash. Too close-minded. And he certainly had all the signs of being domineering and controlling. And God knew she'd had enough of that kind of behavior to last her a lifetime.

She was really tempted to teach the arrogant accountant a thing or two. She was also just plain tempted, period. Despite all the reasons why she shouldn't be.

After hanging up the phone, Rick only stayed in the Inner View office long enough to read the contents of the file on this Mr. Potter he was impersonating. Luckily the information supplied was brief and sketchy. No age or personal notations. Just a work history and a résumé from which Rick copied down the pertinent details in a small notebook he kept tucked inside his back pocket. He would have loved to hurry things along by making use of the handy-dandy copying machine standing three feet away from him, but decided that the resultant flash from the machine as it was working was too risky.

Rick's handwritten notes were brief, concise, and illegible to anyone but him as he wrote down a job description of Mr. Potter's current position with MolTech Industries as controller and director of finance. Quickly replacing the papers exactly as he found them, Rick figured he now knew all there was to know about Mr. Potter. Well, enough to get by with, anyway...including the fact that Potter's first name was Richard. A lucky break. One of many Rick was determined to make happen on this case. Because he was a man who believed in making his own luck.

"Dannazióne!" Holly swore in Italian as yet another potential masterpiece on the potter's wheel collapsed inward on itself. She'd almost made it. The piece had grown upward and taken shape...until she'd been momentarily distracted by thoughts of Rick, and in the blink of an eye disaster had struck.

Tired of rocking on her front porch and brooding about Rick, Holly had come over to the art studio to try once again to successfully throw a pot. Instead she felt like throwing her work into the nearest garbage bin. She added another curse in Cantonese before giving up for the night. It was late. Time to quit.

The light treble sound of the wind chimes on her front porch guided her through the darkness back to her cabin. While walking, she was mentally reviewing the list of art supplies for her shopping trip into Tacoma tomorrow. And while in town, she wouldn't be able to resist picking up one of her favorite chocolate mousse pies, the one with the seven different kinds of chocolate. Talk about temptation....

Naturally, temptation got her to thinking about Rick again. He really wasn't her type. So why did he get to her? Was it those sinful blue eyes of his? Or that wicked grin....

By the time she finally noticed that there was someone standing in the path in front of her, it was too late to avoid walking right into him. It was Rick. Again.

"Crikey!" she muttered in exasperation. "We've got to stop meeting like this."

"Crikey?" Rick repeated.

"An English expression I picked up from a friend of mine," Holly explained.

"You seem to have a lot of friends," he noted.

"I've been lucky that way."

"What about your family?"

"My friends *are* my family," she stated.

"You don't have any family of your own?" he asked.

"I'm not married," she replied.

"That's not what I asked you," Rick pointed out.

"No, but you were going to." Holly saucily tossed his own words back at him.

Rick already knew she wasn't married and never had been. He knew all the facts and statistics about Holly, from her birth date to her weight. Now he needed to know the right buttons to push to get her to go home to Daddy.

Rick was good with women. He was confident that he could sweet-talk Holly, flighty debutante that she was reputed to be, into returning home. Once she got there, it was up to her father to keep her there. Rick's job would be done.

"What about your *real* family?" he asked.

"What about them?"

"Are they some kind of taboo subject or something?" Rick inquired mockingly. "Is that why you're avoiding the question?"

"I wasn't avoiding the question," she denied. Then her innate honesty made her add, "Okay, so maybe I was avoiding the question just a bit."

"You don't get along well with your family?"

"I don't get along well with my father, and since he's the only blood relative I have, I guess that means I don't get along well with my family. You make it sound as if I don't get along with an entire group of people, though, and that's not the case. My father is only one man, although he likes to think of himself as God." She shifted uneasily, taking a step away from Rick. "How did we get on this subject, anyway?"

"I asked you about your family."

"Well, ask me something else."

Holly watched as a flying insect the size of a small cargo plane abruptly dive-bombed Rick. She smiled at his typical city-dweller reaction of ducking. His hasty movement brought his lips within very close range of hers . . . and suddenly she wasn't smiling anymore.

The next thing Holly knew, he was kissing her. One minute she was amused by his actions, the next she was aroused. She hadn't seen this coming. She wasn't prepared for the tantalizing feel of his mouth consuming hers.

Holly closed her eyes and saw images. A figurine she'd picked up from a trip to Holland. A boy and a girl. Kissing. With magnetic lips. Hands behind their backs. Mouths fused with an irrefutable force.

As if unintentionally mirroring the pose of that figurine, Holly had her hands clutched behind her back. She squeezed her fingers together to stop them from giving in to temptation and reaching out to wander over to his body. It didn't do any good.

Like a curious cat, she just had to explore. She touched his chest. The warmth of his body radiated through the cotton of his sweatshirt, a handful of which she wrinkled as she clenched her fingers with feline appreciation at the tactile pleasure.

Their kiss went on. It was a revelation. Holly had never felt this way before. On some distant level she recognized the fact that his hands were sliding down her back, over the smooth denim of her orange jeans to the curve of her derriere, where he cupped her and lifted her against him. The contact was electrifying.

"Let's . . . mmm . . . let's finish this inside—" Rick's tongue darted inside her parted lips to tantalize her further. "Inside your cabin," he murmured without completely lifting his lips from hers.

"What do you mean?" Holly's brain was still pleasantly fuzzy and his intentions simply weren't sinking into her consciousness.

"We can't go back to my cabin," Rick said. "It's already overcrowded as it is. And there's only a twin bed. I hope your bed is bigger than a twin, honey."

Instantly, Holly's rationality returned and with it her strength, which she used to great effectiveness as she angrily shoved Rick away from her. "Nothing could be bigger than your ego if you think I'm going to bed with you, buster!"

Four

———

"**W**hat are you so upset about?" Rick demanded.

"Your arrogant assumption that just because I let you kiss me—"

"Hey, you were kissing me back!" he inserted.

"Fine. Just because I returned your kiss, that doesn't mean that I... that you... that we..."

"Spit it out."

"If you think that we're going to make love after just one kiss—"

"How many kisses will it take?" Rick interrupted her. "I'm willing."

"I'm not," she informed him.

"You were a minute ago."

"I was willing to kiss you. There is a big difference between that and sleeping with you! I don't make love with every man I kiss."

"Glad to hear that. Wise decision, given the number of incurable social diseases these days."

"My point exactly."

"So is this the part where we swap medical records?" he mockingly inquired.

"No, it's the part where you go back to your cabin and I go back to mine."

"Until next time."

His self-assurance irritated her. "Sounds like you have more confidence than brains, Rick. Considering the fact that you're a numbers whiz, one would think you have plenty of brains . . . which means your confidence level has to be right off the map."

"Clear off the map," he cheerfully agreed.

Holly shook her head in amazement. "You know, you're proud of the damnedest things. Like the fact that you're insensitive and overly self-confident."

"I never said I was overly self-confident."

"No, *I* said that."

"You're wrong."

"Really? There's a meaningful saying about self-confidence—"

"Comes from some obscure Tibetan monk, no doubt."

"Actually, it's from former Pittsburgh Steelers football coach Chuck Noll. And it goes like this: Empty barrels make the most noise."

"Ah, but I don't make a lot of noise," Rick seductively countered. "I walk softly...and carry a very, very big stick."

Holly couldn't resist grinning. "Yes, I had noticed that," she sassily retorted, undaunted by his innuendo. "However, it's time you and your very, very big stick walked softly back to your own cabin."

His answering grin took her breath away. "You've got a sense of humor." He sounded surprised by the discovery. "I like that in a woman."

"You've got too much self-confidence. I *don't* like that in a man."

"You prefer your men meek and mild?"

"I prefer them enlightened."

"Enlightened—as in totally emasculated, practically castrated."

"We only use castration as a last resort," Holly noted with a perfectly straight face.

"That reassures me no end."

"I thought it might. Good night, Rick."

Nice going, Dunbar, he mockingly congratulated himself as he watched Holly lightly sprint up the steps to her cabin. You make it to bat and hit nothing but strikes.

The lady threw a hell of a curveball. Hell of a fastball, too, Rick added—remembering the swift and instant heat of their kiss. He hadn't planned on this happening. But now that it had, he wasn't about to walk away from the challenge.

As it stood now, the current score was fancy lady, two; private investigator, still zero, in the bottom of the first inning. Eight innings, and eight days, left to go. Only then would Rick start to worry.

For some reason, Holly dreamed about baseball that night. She'd never dreamed about a game before. She'd have to check with Skye to see what it might mean. Skye knew a lot about interpreting dreams.

Since Holly hadn't gotten much sleep last night, she chose something especially bright and cheerful to wear. Not that she had many dull things in her closet. She'd long ago banished beiges and grays, as well as most black-and-white items. And no plaids, since many of her boarding-school uniforms had been plaid of one sort or another. Plaids gave her the willies.

The freedom to dress in splashes of color was just part of a morning ritual that Holly enjoyed. This was one of the favorite parts of her day, when she did her daily yoga and meditation session.

Afterward, Holly tossed aside her cotton sleepshirt, her days-of-the-week underwear and her Rocky and Bullwinkle socks before stepping into the shower. The humidity immediately made her wavy hair go berserk. Consequently she felt like the Wild Woman of Borneo as she got dressed in a pair of ultrablue leggings with an oversize hot pink T-shirt that almost reached her knees. The multicolored sash she tied around her waist had been handwoven by Skye and picked up both the color of Holly's leggings and T-shirt. Her socks were hot pink as were her high-topped gym shoes.

From her eccentric collection of jewelry, Holly added a woven necklace comprised of Guatemalan worry dolls and her silver chime earrings designed to duplicate the wind chimes she had hanging from her front porch.

Unable to put it off any longer, Holly had to deal with her hair—which she did by brushing it gently and leaving it loose around her shoulders, then tying it away from her face with a neon shoelace in electric blue. Her makeup—made from natural ingredients—was the "lick and a promise" version—eyeshadow and lip gloss in matching shades of dusty rose and a smidgen of mascara. A few dabs of all-natural, lemon-scented body cream, and she was done. Total time spent: five minutes.

Holly lingered over her breakfast of several slices of Skye's homemade bread toasted and generously heaped with orange-pineapple-cherry marmalade. A mug of mellow English breakfast tea, flavored with milk and honey, completed her favorite morning menu. On her way out of the cabin, Holly shredded a remaining crust of bread and tossed the pieces to the birds—a bold gray jay and a few chickadees—before heading for the main office.

Charity was there waiting for her.

"How's the baby this morning? Everything still okay?" Holly asked, having checked with Charity on more than one occasion the previous evening.

"Yes, her fever is down. She sure gave me a scare, though."

"I know. It's not easy being a mom, is it?"

"That's for sure. But it wasn't easy being an exotic dancer in Arizona, either, and I survived. I gotta tell you again how glad I am that you offered me this job," Charity said. "I couldn't have lasted much longer at that sleazy bar."

Holly had stopped at the Blue Bar for lunch, not realizing its name didn't refer to its color scheme. "The bar may have been sleazy . . . but you're a talented dancer."

"Thanks. Unfortunately the guys in that bar weren't there to see my talents as a dancer. And then after Billy Jo lit into me when I told him I was pregnant . . . I don't know what I would have done if you hadn't come along when you did."

Holly gave the younger woman a comforting hug. "Hey, you're family now, Charity."

"I'm not sure everyone here has accepted my past as easily as you have."

"What do you mean?"

"Byron. He never looks at me when he speaks to me. And he hardly ever speaks to me."

"Byron would never place judgment on someone, Charity. He's not like that."

"I want him to like me. I mean, I want to fit in." Charity seemed uncomfortable all of a sudden, as if she'd inadvertently revealed too much already. She quickly changed the subject. "Oh, I forgot to tell you that the office was unlocked this morning when I got here."

"*Helvete,*" Holly swore in Swedish. "I bet I forgot to lock up last night, what with everything that was going on. You didn't find anything missing, did you? The computer and the copying machine are still here?'' Holly quickly checked for their presence.

"They're still here," Charity reassured her. "Nothing is missing, as far as I can tell. Even the papers on my desk weren't rearranged. By the way, I see that Mr. Potter checked in.''

"Rick Potter. Yes, he showed up yesterday afternoon. Missed the orientation session, but then he seems like a fast learner." *And a fast mover, given the speed with which Rick had kissed her!*

Holly caught herself wondering how he was doing with the day's classes. She imagined him sitting there, probably lazily leaning back in his chair, feet stuck out straight in front of him, arms crossed over his chest. A typically arrogant and recalcitrant male posture.

Rick was indeed making himself comfortable as he semi-listened to and semi-ignored Sharon's discussion of creative problem solving. Hell, he didn't see what the big deal was with this problem-solving stuff. In his book, if you had a problem, you dealt with it. Got rid of it. Fired it. Dumped it. Moved on. What did creativity have to do with it?

The topic of problems naturally got Rick to thinking about Holly and what he'd learned about her so far. Number one: That she disliked her father. Big surprise, he noted mockingly. Had Holly and her old man gotten along, there would have been no need for Rick to have been called in. Number two: That her kisses were dynamite and she felt like a custom-fit in his arms.

He'd moved too fast last night. He hadn't been thinking clearly. Sweet-talking her into going back to her father was one thing. Sleeping with her was something else entirely.

Despite the carte blanche Old Man Redmond had given him, Rick had no illusions about the reasons for that approval. Redmond was looking out for his own best interests. It was up to Rick to look out for *his* own best interests. Which meant keeping his mind on his job…and, of course, on that five thousand waiting to be collected once he'd accomplished his goals.

In the end, business and pleasure never mixed successfully. Rick knew that from watching other people mess up. The bottom line, as far as he was concerned, was getting the job done. He just had to decide the best way of doing that.

Much as he hated to admit it, Rick was quickly realizing that getting Holly to do something against her will wasn't going to be the piece of cake he first thought it would be. For one thing, she was incredibly stubborn. And too damn independent for any woman's good. So far, his attempts at sweet-talking her had been shot down in flames…and just ended up making him want to take her in his arms and kiss her senseless.

The problem was that she challenged him. Everything about her was a challenge—from her sassy, sexy walk to her irreverent sense of humor. His first attempt at charming her had resulted in her bluntly informing him that she preferred him when he was telling her the truth.

The truth. Rick wearily wondered if he even knew what that was anymore.

He shifted uncomfortably. This was no time to start reevaluating his approach to life, and he resented Holly for making him question things. What did she, coddled in the finest boarding schools most of her life, know about the realities of life?

She'd never had to fight for anything in her life. He had. Nothing had come easily for him. Including this case. But he always got the job done in the end. And that's all that mattered. He'd get this job done, too.

"I can't do that. I don't know how," eight-year-old Jordan staunchly stated.

"You can learn how, Jordan," Holly said.

"No, I can't," the boy maintained.

"Why not?"

"'Cause I'm not smart."

"Says who?"

"My teacher and the kids at school. They say I'm a dummy."

Holly had heard the words before. They'd been applied to her by a particularly cruel headmistress when she'd been a year or two older than Jordan was now. She'd also heard the words from the other children she'd been working with over the course of the summer.

Some of the children came to her via the county human services agencies. Some had come because of word-of-mouth recommendations. Most were being raised by single moms who spent their days trying to make a living for themselves and their kids. Some of the children stayed at the camp in the log cabins, with Skye and her husband acting as dorm parents. Some were picked up by their moms every evening. All were here for the same reason.

They needed help. They needed someone to care. Someone to give them hope and make them feel good about themselves.

That's where Holly fit in. She was proud of the program they'd developed here at Inner View. She'd gotten her bachelor's degree in early childhood education, yet another thing that had angered her father. He'd wanted her to be a business major and had immediately cut off her college payments. She'd been halfway through her freshman year at the time. Scholarship money had been tough to get given her father's financial status, but she'd managed by working part-time as a waitress and living in a loft with six other people to share expenses.

After graduation she'd had a brief stint as a third-grade teacher in San Francisco, but the lack of funds in the inner-city school, as well as the idiotic, restrictive rules, had soon disillusioned her. She could still remember her principal's response to her heated request for updated books for her students—"These kids can't read, anyway. Why get them new books?"

For the next four years Holly had tried her hand at a number of things. She'd known that her father hadn't approved of what he called her "footloose ways." He wanted her to return home and join the family import-export business in Seattle so that he could groom her to take over one day.

But Holly was determined *not* to follow in her father's footsteps. Unlike her father, she made people—not material things—the number-one priority in her life.

Which is how she'd ended up where she was, working with her class of seven- and eight-year-olds. Right now, Holly had the four neediest kids to herself while Skye worked with the others in her workshop, teaching them weaving techniques. Jordan was one of the needy ones.

"I don't think you're a dummy, Jordan," Holly reassured him. "And this isn't a school here. We're just fooling around and experimenting by drawing and painting and making things. We're explorers. We play here, Jordan."

"You don't even have any video games here," Jordan scoffed. "How can you play without video games? Or even a TV."

"Easily. Watch us and join in. You, too, Martha," Holly added for the benefit of the painfully shy little girl with the big blue eyes. Martha constantly tweaked her long blond hair, which kept her left hand busy at all times. "You know, the reason I like art is because there's no right or wrong way—only your way."

"If there's no right or wrong way, how come you wouldn't let us paint Martha's hair with our paints yesterday?" precocious Larry demanded.

"Because Martha didn't want to have her hair painted," Holly replied.

"I wanted *my* hair painted," Bobby stated. Bobby was the great experimenter, a hyperactive child.

"Me, too. I wanted my hair painted, too," Jordan piped up, clearly wanting to fit in.

"Maybe next time. Right now we're going to look in a mirror."

"A mirror?" Jason repeated. "What for?"

"To see what you'd look like with green hair probably," Larry inserted.

Holly said, "You know those pictures I showed you yesterday? The ones I have posted on the board over there with all the different self-portraits people have done?" She'd included examples by Rembrandt, Van Gogh and Picasso, among others.

"I like the one of the guy who cut off his ear," Bobby declared. "I bet it bled a lot. I cut my ear once and gallons of blood came gushing out of me and splattered all over the walls."

Holly noticed that Martha was tweaking her hair with both hands now.

"How about all of you doing a self-portrait of yourselves?" Holly quickly suggested, diverting their attention. Self-portraits were one of the best indicators of how children saw themselves in terms of self-esteem. Tiny hands could denote a feeling of helplessness, while a small mouth might indicate that a child felt what they said wasn't important.

"I don't want to," Jordan said. "I don't know how."

"I'll show you," Holly replied. "Look in the mirror and tell me what you see." She held it up for him.

"I see me," Jordan replied.

"Right. Now all you have to do is draw what you see. You remember our talk about curves and lines and circles and squares?"

"I like those squished circles," Larry inserted.

"Ovals," Holly said.

"Yeah. My face is an oval." Larry drew an oval on his piece of paper and triumphantly held it aloft. "There! I did it! I'm an artist!"

Larry's enthusiasm spread to the other three, who began experimenting with the shape of their faces as they studied themselves in their hand mirrors.

By the end of their session, each child had completed a drawing. Bobby's self-portrait had only one ear, which was placed on top of his head. Martha's portrait had stick-figure arms and legs with small hands—the thumb was stuck in her mouth. Larry's self-portrait looked like something Picasso might have done. And Jordan...Jordan's self-portrait looked the most lifelike and he was clearly delighted with it.

"I guess I'm not such a dummy after all, huh?" he murmured.

The process of healing had started. Holly blinked back the tears as she ruffled his hair with her hand. "That's right, Jordan. You're not a dummy at all. None of you are."

Rick saw Holly before she saw him. The screen gently blurred her features, giving her a softness around the edges that was endearing. Rick immediately caught himself. What the hell was wrong with him, coming up with a stupid observation like that?

He watched her ruffling the hair of a small boy, noting the way the kid beamed up at her appreciatively. So she was good with kids. So what? That didn't mean anything.

At thirty-four, Rick had seen enough of the seedy side of life to stop believing in the basic goodness of man or woman—or even child, for that matter. He'd long ago lost faith in happy endings, if he'd ever believed in them in the first place. He refused to be moved by the scene before him.

Holly looked up and saw Rick. He was frowning at her. She wondered what his problem was now. She gave him an exaggerated frown in return and then smiled at him. "What are you doing standing there?"

"They let us loose for twenty minutes," Rick replied.

"You make it sound like you broke out of prison."

"That's how it feels."

"Are you really a prisoner?" Bobby demanded through the screen, running over to join Holly. "My dad's in prison. You know him? His name is—"

"I was just kidding," Rick hurriedly stated.

"Rick isn't really a prisoner," Holly confirmed. "He's an accountant."

With that news, the children quickly lost interest in him, Holly was amused to note. She wished she could do the same, but no such luck. "You might as well come in and join us."

Rick didn't need a second invitation. He sat there and watched as Holly worked with the kids. Once more he was struck by how utterly expressive her face was. Not only her eyes, which lit up with enthusiasm, but her mouth...

He spent a good five minutes fantasizing about her mouth. Remembering the feel, the texture, the taste of it. And hungering for a second helping.

He didn't even notice the kids had left until Holly snapped her fingers in front of him. "Thinking about spreadsheets, were you?" she teased him.

The only thing he wanted spread on a sheet was her. Naked. So he could kiss every inch of her.

"You don't really feel like a prisoner here, do you?" she asked.

"A paying prisoner."

"Stop complaining. Your employer could have sent you to one of those adventure/learning courses. The kind where you build trust by climbing up a fifty-foot wall studded with pegs and the participants are attached to each other with bungee cords."

"What's that supposed to be? Some new way for the boss to *terminate* you? Certainly gives new meaning to the term."

Holly laughed at his sardonic comment. "It's supervised, and care is taken with safety. But you have to coordinate your movements with the others on your team or you won't get very far. It's sort of a rite of passage designed to teach people—including bosses—that it's okay to take risks."

"I take risks all the time."

"It's not just risk-taking. It's a matter of having faith. Of being part of a team."

"Faith? That's for cowards and idiots. Just be willing to accept reality and stop kidding yourself. Everybody is out for themselves. That's the bottom line. Basically, people are no damn good. You accept that and you're ahead of the game."

"No way. I don't agree with you at all. There are plenty of good people in the world. The trick is finding them, or letting them find you."

"I'll bet you believe in Santa Claus and the Tooth Fairy, too, right?"

"Absolutely," she confirmed with a grin, not the least bit insulted by his sarcasm. "Don't you?"

"Just kid stories to me," Rick replied. "And I don't believe in happy endings, either. I can't remember a time when I did."

"That's so sad."

"Yeah, I'm a real sad case," Rick drawled mockingly.

"Mmm," Holly agreed. "Unenlightened, overconfident, insensitive and now a disbeliever in happy endings who thinks people are no damn good." She shook her head. "You're gonna take a lot of work."

"What's that supposed to mean?" he demanded suspiciously.

"Just that I think there's something in you worth redeeming. Call me crazy, but I'm not ready to give up on you just yet."

"Should I be flattered?"

"Certainly. You should be awed and humbled by my interest."

"Yeah, right. I'm *interested* in your interest. That mean we're ready to resume where we left off in front of your cabin the other night?"

"No, it most definitely does not! My interest is strictly professional."

"Liar," he said softly. "Your interest is very personal."

"Your ego is showing again." Reaching out, she placed her hand over his mouth. "And before you tell me that you'd like to show me a lot more than your ego, I should remind you that..."

The feel of his tongue on the inner heart of her palm chased all thought of what she was going to say right out of her mind.

Disconcerted, she pulled her hand away.

Looking at her and grinning wickedly, Rick murmured, "You should remind me of what?"

"Nothing. You already know more than you should," she muttered, amazed at the way her hand was still humming. You'd think the guy was wired for 220 volts or something!

"Still think I need work?" he inquired.

"Definitely."

"And you think you're woman enough for the job?"

"Oh, I'm woman enough, all right. The question is, are you man enough?"

"Is that a challenge? You want me to prove that I'm man enough?"

"Sure. Prove you're man enough . . . by taking my drawing class tomorrow afternoon. You've got a free period of about an hour. Spend it here."

Catching her hand in his, he slid his fingers between hers in a slow slide that was surprisingly erotic. "Offering me private lessons, are you?"

"No. I'm offering you a chance to recapture your childhood."

"No, thanks." Releasing her, Rick abruptly stepped away. "There's nothing I want to recapture from my childhood."

"Was it that bad?" she asked softly.

Rick knew then that this was the way to get to her. This was the button to push to gain Holly's trust. So why was he hesitating to use it? His own instinctive reaction had always been to resent anyone feeling sorry for him. Yet here was his chance to finally make some headway with Holly. He needed to take advantage of her compassionate sympathy. He had a job to do here, damn it!

"Bad?" he repeated. "Not unless you call having your mother die when you're thirteen and your dad drinking himself to death 'bad.'"

"I'm sorry. My mother died when I was eight," Holly admitted slowly. "There are times when I still miss her, even though I can't remember exactly what she looked like. My father burned all her pictures when she died."

"My dad did the same thing."

"Yeah?"

"Yeah." For once, Rick wasn't lying. Granted, there had only been a few cheap snapshots of her. His dad's drinking habit had used up any extra spending they might have. Used up food and rent money sometimes, too. Certainly no money for film or a halfway decent camera. Now even those few pictures were gone. Along with Rick's faith in happy endings.

"I guess we have something in common after all," Holly noted quietly.

"I guess we do," he agreed, wondering why he still felt a twinge of guilt when he hadn't even lied. He was finally making progress. He should be celebrating.

Noticing his frown, Holly asked, "Is something wrong?"

"Nothing I can't fix," Rick muttered.

"Your break is over," she told him, glancing at her Van Gogh watch. "I'm glad we had this talk." Her voice was rich with earnest warmth, blanketing his soul.

Hold the phone here! Rick shook his head as if clearing his thoughts from the grips of a hangover. Baiting the flighty rich girl who'd always gotten everything she wanted was one thing. Teasing her, riling her—hell, even kissing her—was fine. But letting her get under his skin was completely out of the question.

He was probably just tired. After all, he hadn't gotten much sleep last night. The damn trees had kept him awake, not to mention the steamy memories of Holly's kiss. Yeah, that had to be it. He was tired. She wasn't getting under his skin. That self-diagnosis made, Rick immediately felt much better.

"I'm glad we had this talk, too," he said. Because he'd gotten a lot accomplished. He'd softened her up without getting softened up in the process. A good day's work. He'd do well to remember that . . . and the five-thousand-dollar check waiting to be collected in Seattle upon her return.

Five

———

That night, Rick was feeling restless—the damn trees were making noise again—so he went out walking...*stalking* was actually more like it. Unfortunately, he didn't run into Holly again as he had the night before. Too bad. He'd had a hunger for another one of her kisses. Not that it wasn't a hunger he couldn't control. Rick prided himself on being in control, among other things.

The camp was dark and quiet, as it had been last night. It was only a little after ten. You'd think it was the middle of the night instead of just the beginning of it, Rick noted, disgruntled.

Then he heard it, the sound of male laughter. Curiosity got the better of him and he moseyed on over to check it out. The noise was coming from one of the smaller cabins. The front door was open and he could see the inhabitants clearly through the screen door—Whit, Guido and the guy in the wheelchair...Byron, Rick corrected himself.

For the first time, Rick noticed that Byron's black hair was actually quite long and was gathered in a braid. He realized then that he hadn't really seen Byron before. He'd only seen his wheelchair; not that Rick had paid a lot of attention to that, either, preoccupied as he was with getting away from the big-mouthed little redheaded girl.

"Come on in, Rick," Byron suddenly called out.

The guy had to have great night vision to have seen him out here, Rick noted, duly impressed.

He was even more impressed by the pile of cash in front of Byron at the table. "What's your game, guys?" Rick asked.

"What's *your* game?" Guido countered.

Hooking his foot around the leg of a folding chair, Rick sat down and expertly shuffled the deck of cards. "My game? Seven-card stud. One-eyed jacks and red threes are wild. We open with jacks or better. That okay with you boys?"

"You didn't ask about stakes," Byron pointed out.

"Five bucks a game," Guido said.

"I can afford that," Rick stated.

"To go to your favorite charity, not in your pocket," Byron added.

Rick *was* his favorite charity. "Yeah, sure. Whatever. So are we gonna play here or chat?"

"I don't know if it's wise to play cards with a number cruncher," Guido growled. "He might have some kind of mathematical system or something."

"I don't have a mathematical system," Rick replied. His skills at this game were purely instinctive.

"Like you're gonna admit it if you did," Guido retorted. "Where did you say you worked?"

"MolTech," Rick replied easily. "Come on, guys, what's the problem here? I'm only interested in a friendly little game of poker. What's the big deal?"

"I got the impression you're not just interested in poker," Guido maintained. "You're interested in something—make that *someone*—else."

"Would you give me a break?" Rick protested with a good-natured smile. "Can't we just have a little R and R and concentrate on the game? You keep coming up with excuses and you boys are gonna have me thinking you're afraid to ante up here."

"I, for one, welcome the challenge of relieving you of some of your money," Byron stated.

"Me, too," Guido growled. "Deal the cards."

"I'm telling you, Rick doesn't look like any accountant I ever saw," Holly noted.

"Now, Holly, you know better than to judge a book by its cover," Skye gently chastised her.

"Yeah, but his cover looks *real* good!" Holly couldn't resist stating.

"I suppose . . . if you like the brash type," Skye said.

"Usually I don't. I prefer men who are tall, dark and talkative." Holly had to admit that Rick was all three of the above. He certainly had a mouth on him . . . a wickedly curved mouth that raised kissing to new levels of pleasure. Holly took too large a sip of tea and almost scalded her mouth. *"Ach du leiber Gott!"* she swore in German.

"You okay?" Skye asked in concern.

"Fine," she muttered, sliding a cooling bite of chocolate mousse pie into her mouth. She'd driven the hour's trip each way earlier that evening and picked up her favorite dessert, along with some art supplies and her jelly beans.

"You were saying that Rick's type doesn't usually interest you, but . . . ?" Skye prompted her.

"But there's something about the man that drives me nuts."

"His after-shave?" Skye teasingly suggested.

"He doesn't wear any."

"So you've noticed that small detail about him."

"There's something more to this guy than meets the eye—although, as I said, what meets the eye is mighty fine," Holly added with an irrepressible grin.

"You've met handsome guys before," Skye pointed out. "Even had a few fall for you, as I recall. And you couldn't have cared less."

"I know." Holly sighed and ate another bite of pie. "How do you explain chemistry? You don't. You just run in the other direction."

"Why? What are you afraid of?"

"Of caring for him. Of getting hurt."

"If he hurt you, Guido would be very upset," Skye pointed out.

Holly looked nonplussed. "You don't think Guido said anything to him, do you?"

Skye shrugged. "You know Guido. He's very protective of you."

"He promised he'd stop being so protective."

"Yeah, well he promised he'd stop eating ice cream, too, but I don't see him doing that, either," Skye noted.

"You don't see who doing what?" Guido asked as he entered Holly's cabin with the rest of the guys.

"You refraining from eating ice cream," Holly replied, noting that Rick was right behind Byron. She wondered what he was up to now. There had to be a reason for his tagging along with her friends.

"I've cut down my intake," Guido was telling her.

"If you knew what all that fat does to your body..." Skye inserted.

"I don't want to know," Guido interrupted her. "And besides, since when is chocolate mousse pie nonfattening?"

"We cut the pie into pieces and let the calories out," Holly told Guido.

"So how much did you lose tonight?" Skye asked her husband, Whit.

"Twenty bucks. Decided to send it to Habitat for Humanity this time."

"What about you, Rick?" Holly asked. "How much did you lose?"

"What makes you think I lost anything?" Rick countered.

"Because I know how good Byron is at playing poker."

"I broke even," Rick stated.

Holly raised an eyebrow. "That's a first. How did you hear about their game, anyway?"

"Byron invited me."

"Byron, since when have you started fleecing our participants by inviting them to play poker with you?" Holly teasingly admonished him.

"Hey," Byron protested, "the guy was standing there looking forlorn and I took pity on him."

"Yeah, right," Rick said. "I will say this—every Wednesday night I play poker with the guys back home. Men only. It's great. Just like tonight. Men only."

"Only because they've banned me from their game," Holly said.

"Why's that? You drive them crazy with your questions? Or couldn't you grasp the concept of the game?" Rick mockingly inquired.

"You want to tell him or should I?" Holly asked Byron.

"We banned her because she beat the pants off us," Byron obligingly stated.

"She's welcome to try and beat the pants off me anytime she desires," Rick murmured.

"She doesn't desire," Holly retorted.

"Sure about that?" he countered.

"Positive."

"We'll see."

"That's right. *You'll* see," Holly prophesied as she got to her feet. "In the meantime, I'm going to go make another pot of tea."

"I'll come with you," Rick said.

"There's no need . . ."

Too late. Rick was right behind her as she entered the kitchen. "Oh, there's a need all right, Holly."

"Which has nothing to do with making tea, I'm sure," she retorted. "Your needs are your problem, Rick."

"What about your needs?"

"They're doing just fine, thank you. Don't worry yourself one little bit about them. A piece of my favorite chocolate mousse pie always cures whatever ails me."

"There are more enjoyable ways of curing what ails you."

Instead of backing away, Holly turned and confronted him. "You know, you're right," she murmured in a deliberately seductive come-hither voice.

"I am?" First off, he couldn't believe she was agreeing with him. And secondly, the hungry way she was eyeing him was enough to blow his fuses.

"Sure. German chocolate cake also cures what ails me," she breezily added.

He'd been had. Seeing the self-satisfied gleam in her eyes, Rick surprisingly didn't mind being strung along. Was she for real? Did she really feel things as intensely as she appeared to? Did she really get such pleasure out of little things, like besting him on occasion? If it was an act, she was damn good at it. If it wasn't . . . Intrigued, he watched her as she bustled around the kitchen.

Rick was a good observer. In his line of work, he had to be. And he'd observed that some people liked showing off how smart or how cultured they were when going through the rituals of making coffee. He imagined making tea would be even more ritualistic to that kind of person.

But Holly clearly had no interest in proving anything to anyone. That was evident in everything she did, including making tea. Gathering a handful of loose tea in that graceful hand of hers, she casually tossed it into the teapot.

He'd noticed the teapot before, and it too said something about Holly. He'd never seen another teapot quite like it, not that he was an expert by any means. But then, one tended to remember a pot shaped like a pink hippo—complete with lushly painted black eyelashes and a white bow on one ear. No doubt about it, this woman definitely had her own way of doing things.

Rick wondered how she did other things, like making love. Did she use the same creativity in bed? The same dash of irreverent humor? The same passion for life? The same willingness to experiment? The same freedom?

The possibilities had Rick stifling a groan.

"How strong do you like it?" Holly earnestly asked him.

Rick blinked, momentarily afraid she might have added mind reading to her list of unusual traits. "What did you say?"

"Your tea," she clarified. "How strong do you like it?"

"With a few shots of whiskey in it," he muttered.

"I don't have any whiskey, and even if I did, I certainly wouldn't ruin one of Skye's special blends with it," Holly indignantly stated. The intensity of the look he was giving her made her nervous, so she kept talking. "That's one of the nice things about tea, you know. There are something like three thousand varieties, so you never become bored with it. It's really an ancient art form."

He imagined three thousand varieties of another ancient art form—sex. And sharing them all with her.

Holly felt his eyes on her, and it didn't take a mind reader to get the drift of his thoughts. His gaze was intimate without being insulting, scorching her as surely as the hot tea had earlier. Had any other man looked at her with such dark passion, she wouldn't have felt this way... all unsettled and churning inside...and, even worse, enjoying it. Like white-river rafting and hang gliding combined. Holly had tried both. Uplifting and stimulating, exciting and exhilarating—the descriptions covered her current jumble of emotions.

It was as if she were trapped, entangled in his gaze, held captive by the silent messages flickering from his eyes to hers. The shadowy blue of his eyes had darkened with the intensity of his gaze. They were mesmerizing, and she felt herself being drawn in...closer and closer.

The sound of the shrieking teakettle echoed the shrieking of her nerves. Startled by the noise, Holly jumped before hurriedly turning off the stove.

Rick still didn't say a word. She could feel him watching her as she poured the boiling water into the teapot. She had to say something to break the unbearable silence. Her mind floundered for something to say before latching on to the teapot before her. She pointed to it, hoping to draw his attention away from her. "Nifty teapot, huh? I found it at a flea market in Colorado. Interesting things, teapots. They were developed during the Ming dynasty in the early 1500s. Some people collect them, you know. Potters and ceramic artists have major shows focusing on them."

To her dismay, Rick continued focusing on her.

"I'll bet you've always wondered how people got started drinking this stuff, huh?" she nervously rambled on. "Well, the legend goes that a branch from a tea bush accidentally fell into water being boiled for the Chinese emperor Shen Neng. He was reported to have been delighted by its fragrance and taste, and voilà—" she snapped her fingers "—tea drinking was born."

"You're a regular walking encyclopedia," Rick noted mockingly.

And he was a regular walking minefield, she irritably thought to herself. Actually, she was glad to be irritated with him. She much preferred it to the quicksandy feelings she'd had a few moments ago. When he was annoying, she could deal with him.

"Here." She shoved a tray with the teapot on it toward him. "Since you're here, you might as well be useful."

"Bossy, aren't you?"

"Only when I have to be." One thing Holly knew she'd have to be around Rick was cautious. She was supposed to be teaching him a lesson, not vice versa. The problem was that Rick, like chocolate, was one vice she was finding hard to resist.

Holly only taught one of the business management seminars, the one focusing on creativity exercises. This was the first time Rick was in her session. She'd noted that Rick did indeed sit the way she thought he would—arms crossed on his chest with his hands tucked in against his sides, legs outstretched and crossed at the ankles. The other businessmen in the session were relaxed, but not that relaxed. Holly wondered if Rick sat at his desk at work that way and found it hard to picture.

At the moment, she'd shifted the group's session outside to the picnic tables near the lake. She was also shifting her attention away from Rick to the subject of her discussion.

"Routine," Holly said, as she walked around the tables. A gentle breeze off the lake ruffled the calf-length skirt of her floral challis dress. It was light blue with tiny pink tulips on it and was one of her favorite finds from a flea market in New York. "It's reassuring but it hinders creativity. It puts your powers of observation to sleep."

Sleep. Rick hadn't gotten much of that last night. He eyed Holly with equal parts of resentment and fascination. How did she manage to look so full of life and enthusiasm at this hour of the morning? It was barely nine o'clock. He vowed to drive into town and get some batteries for his portable radio that evening. Those damn noisy trees weren't going to keep him awake another night. While he was at it, he'd grab a burger in town. He needed to keep up his strength. Up... Rick groaned. Wrong choice of word.

"I had you all come out here to perform an easy exercise," Holly said. "An exercise in creativity."

The thought of performing creative exercises with Holly spurred Rick's arousal.

"I want you all to just sit and focus on the world around you," Holly continued. "Allow your senses to take in the sights, the sounds, the smells. Let it all sink in."

Rick almost groaned aloud. Sinking in... He closed his eyes as he imagined himself sinking into her, imagined her silken body joined with his.

"You okay, Rick?" she asked.

"Yeah," he growled without opening his eyes. "Just fine."

"Closing your eyes is a good idea," she commended him. "Helps you focus more intently on the sounds and smells around you."

Only problem was that he was focusing on *her* smell, the fresh tartness of lemon today. As for sounds, aside from the beating of his own heart, he heard her breathing as she sat down beside him. He heard the sound of her voice as she spoke to another participant. Her voice, like her eyes, was incredibly expressive—reflecting her enthusiasm, her passion, her excitement. She had a siren's voice, the kind that would tempt men to leave their independence behind and come to her as she beckoned them closer. Rick might not know much about mythology, but he sure as hell knew what happened to sailors who allowed themselves to be taken in by a siren. They crashed on the rocks.

"You seem awfully tense, Rick," Holly noted. "You need to relax. Perhaps some breathing exercises would help."

Only one kind of exercise would help what ailed him. The kind that made your breathing even more ragged before your entire body exploded with pleasure.

When she put her hand on his shoulder, Rick almost jumped out of his skin.

Bending to speak to him, she said, "You need to breathe in deeply...."

"I know what I need," he growled for her ears only. "Your mouth on mine. And unless you want me to repeat what happened the other night right here in front of the rest of the class, you better keep your hands to yourself, lady."

He expected her to snatch her hand away with virtuous outrage. Instead she stroked his cheek in a teasingly chiding gesture. "Try and keep your mind on the exercises, Rick."

"You're pushing your luck," he warned her with a dark look.

Smiling, she breezily moved on to the next participant, which had Rick glaring at her. He didn't hear what she said and didn't pay any attention to her damn exercises. He was too damn upset with what was happening to him. This wasn't jealousy he was feeling? For Holly? Just because she paid attention to the engineer with the bald spot? He was definitely losing it. He needed a beer.

Maybe he'd been without a woman for too long. He'd broken up with Liz almost a year ago, and hadn't dated much since. His relationship with Liz had benefitted them both in different ways and had ended when she'd gotten a job promotion that involved a transfer to Singapore. There a banker had swept her off her feet. She'd faxed Rick the announcement that she'd gotten married.

There were times when Rick missed the comfortable arrangement he'd had with Liz. It hadn't been wildly passionate. They hadn't even been in love. But their relationship had filled certain needs, needs that were now running rampant whenever Holly was around.

"I can't stress how important creativity is in developing self-esteem," Holly was saying. "As a child, constant criticism or habitual indifference to your achievements can be very damaging. That's why you're here today—to recapture some of that creative spontaneity we all had as children and free up your inner potential, opening yourself to new possibilities. In many of us that creative spontaneity was squelched at an early age. When that happens a child is burdened with self-doubt and insecurity instead of a sense of confidence."

"You seem pretty confident to me," Rick inserted.

"So do you," Holly retorted. "But appearances can be deceptive. Someone who is very cocky and overly self-confident may actually have very low self-esteem, which they're just covering up by their behavior."

"And how is all this stuff supposed to make us do our job better?" Rick demanded.

"By coming up with new ways of problem solving, new ways of working with others, more effective and therefore faster ways of getting your work done," Holly replied.

"We can do all this by listening to birds?" he scoffed.

"You can do all that by listening *period,* Rick. It's one of the most important skills an executive can have these days. It's a skill you should consider developing." She gave him a meaningful look before turning her attention to the rest of the group and saying, "Thanks, everybody. That does it for my session today. Byron will be starting the next session in fifteen minutes."

"Were you talking about your childhood?" Rick asked her as the others meandered off.

"I was talking about everyone's childhood. If you belittle a child's abilities, throughout their life that child will hear an inner murmur, the echoes of the taunts from their childhood, undermining their self-confidence."

"Yeah, well there are worse things that can happen to a kid than having their dad insult their dumb painting."

"I get the impression you're referring to something specific here. Perhaps in your own life?"

"My life's got nothing to do with it," Rick said.

"Doesn't sound that way to me."

"Is this where you invite me onto your couch?" he inquired mockingly.

"No. It's where you tell me the truth, for a change."

"What does that mean?" Had she somehow guessed what he was up to? Rick wondered.

"It means that you tend to hide behind this scoundrel facade of yours. Behind a wicked grin and a cynical comment."

"Hey, we all have our strengths," he retorted. "Wicked grins and cynical comments just happen to be mine."

"And we all have our weaknesses," Holly added.

"So this is about weaknesses? You looking for mine?"

"You'd rather I thought you didn't have any, wouldn't you?"

"Hey, if it makes you feel better to think I've got weaknesses, go right ahead. I'll be the first to admit I've got a weakness for brown-eyed blondes."

"In that case I'll have to go out and get a pair of those colored contacts right away," she tartly retorted. "Blue, maybe. I always wanted to have blue eyes," she added wistfully. Holly's mother had had blue eyes. She wasn't pleased to have inherited her father's brown eyes.

"Leave your eyes the way they are," Rick practically ordered her.

Holly frowned. "There's something you should know about me, Rick. I don't take orders very well at all."

"Neither do I."

"That much I could guess," she commented wryly.

"I was in the navy and I got enough orders there to last me a lifetime. What's your excuse?" Rick countered.

"A father who thought he was the commander-in-chief. Thank the Lord I'm over twenty-one now and my father can't drag me back into his feudal clutches. I'm safe now. Free."

"Don't you think you're being kind of hard on your dad? What about his feelings?" Rick deliberately played on the usual feelings of guilt a child had about their parents. "What if he misses you?"

"That's *his* problem. I don't give a damn."

The intensity and vehemence of Holly's reply took Rick by surprise. "So you don't care if he lives or dies, is that it?"

"I didn't say that," Holly denied. "Naturally I don't wish him any harm. He *is* my father, after all. But I'm not going to let him use my emotions against me."

"Come on," Rick chided her. "You make him sound like some kind of monster."

"No, he's not a monster. He's a spider—weaving his sticky webs around people, trapping them until they're paralyzed, sapping all the joy and spontaneity out of them until they submissively do his bidding. He wants blind obedience. Always has. Instead he got me, who's neither blind nor obedient. Trust me, we're better off apart."

"How can you know that?"

"Let me put it this way—*I'm* better off staying away from him."

"Would you go see him if he were sick?" Rick said.

"Why all this interest in my father?" she asked suspiciously. "Do you know him or something?"

"No. But I had a father once. Trust me, it's better to make your peace than to have things left unfinished."

"You said your father died."

"I said he drank himself to death. There's a difference."

"You make it sound as if he deliberately drank himself to death."

"He did."

"What makes you say that? Rick, alcoholism is a disease."

"Save the speech," he curtly told her. "I've heard it before."

"Oh, right. I forgot. You're the tough guy who prefers analytical facts to emotional jargon."

"That's me."

"No, that's not really you," she said. "That's my dad. I can tell the difference. Of course, you could use some improving...."

"Thanks a lot."

"...but I don't think you're a lost cause yet, Rick."

In his book, Rick would only be a lost cause if he let Holly get under his skin.

"What's your favorite part of your painting?" Holly asked Bobby during their painting session later that afternoon.

"The green blood," Bobby instantly replied.

"It's very colorful," Holly agreed. "Tell me about your painting."

"I want to tell you about mine," Larry inserted.

"You can tell us about yours next. Go ahead, Bobby."

"This is a mutant radioactive lizard that is going to eat this city in the sky here," Bobby said.

"What's a lizard doing in the sky?" Larry demanded, apparently unperturbed that the city was in the sky.

"It's a flying lizard," an unfazed Bobby replied. "These are its wings. And this over here is the superhero in his spaceship. He's shooting the killer lizard with his laser gun."

"You did a great job with the city," Holly complimented him.

Bobby beamed.

Holly's purpose in asking each child about his or her favorite part of their painting was a deliberate attempt to have the children learn to evaluate their own accomplishments and not be dependent on adults for feelings of self-worth. It was yet another step in the process.

After class, Holly's next task was tidying up her cabin. In particular, Holly wanted to try out the new vacuum cleaner she'd picked up on her jaunt into Tacoma yesterday. Traveling as much as she had over the past few years, it hadn't been practical to own one before, so she'd made do with an electric broom. She was looking forward to having something more powerful to clean with.

Eager to try the vacuum, she decided not to take the time to change out of her calf-length dress. Her mind, however, was not on her work as she vacuumed her way across the living room—over rugs and hardwood floors. Her mind was on Rick, as it had been for a good part of the day.

Sitting next to him during the creative exercise this morning had ended up being nothing more than an exercise in futility. He'd been relatively quiet, not making as many suggestive comments as he'd made in the past. But he'd given her several of what she'd now labeled "those looks." The ones that made her feel like her bones were melting.

Caught up in the memory of the way Rick's eyes had caressed her, Holly undid one of the vacuum's nifty hand-held attachments to clean the corners of the room, which hadn't seen the end of a vacuum in more time than she cared to consider. As she bent down, however, she felt a tug on her skirt. Turning around, she realized that the main part of the vacuum was still sucking. In fact, it had sucked the hem of her skirt right into its rollers!

Dismayed, Holly tried to reach the power button but couldn't locate it on the handle. By now her skirt was thoroughly wrapped up, and the vacuum was not a happy camper. The ominous growl of the engine did not bode well for a long lifetime for this new appliance. She doubted this was doing her dress any good, either!

Frustrated by her inability to turn the stupid appliance off, Holly was yelling "Stop that!" when she heard Rick drawl, "Turning it off is usually more effective than yelling at it."

"You're a big help," she retorted, finally locating the power switch and turning it off.

However, she was still practically joined at the hip with the appliance, which held the skirt of her dress in its rolling jaws. The material was pulled against her hip and the usually long hem was well above the knee on her free side.

"Dangerous work, vacuuming," he mockingly noted.

"What are you doing here?"

"I was just passing by when I heard you yelling. I looked through the screen door and saw you battling with a hungry vacuum cleaner." Reaching over, he unplugged the cord from the wall outlet. "Here, let me help." But instead of helping, he just sat there, eyeing her.

"What do you think you're doing?" Holly breathlessly demanded with far less emphasis than she would have liked.

"Admiring the view," Rick replied.

His lazy drawl burned her blood, but no more so than the heated look he was giving her partially bare legs. "Admire the view of Mount Rainier over the lake. Not of my legs."

"I prefer your legs to the view of Mount Rainier any day."

"I wouldn't aggravate me, if I were you," she warned him.

"Oh? And why's that?"

"Because I'm the owner of a killer vacuum cleaner and I know where you sleep at night."

"Sounds kinky to me," he murmured with that wicked grin of his.

"You wouldn't think so if you were being sucked into a household appliance," she retorted. "Well, maybe you would. God knows what your tastes are in your private leisure activities."

"Well, now that you asked—"

"I didn't," she interrupted him. "Aren't you done yet?" she impatiently demanded, tugging on her still-imprisoned-and-imprisoning skirt.

"I've barely gotten started," he murmured, softly brushing his fingers along the sensitive curve behind her knee. Holly shivered, secretly glad that she'd shaved her legs last night. That strange feeling was happening to her again. That internal humming. The vacuum cleaner had hummed like that in her hand as she'd pushed it across the floor... before she had gotten entangled in it. A subtle vibration. It truly was amazing, and Holly was most impressed by Rick's effect on her.

So she sat there and studied him. Studied him closely. She could see the deep, attractive lines around his mouth when he smiled sideways at her. For the first time, she noticed the way he raised his eyebrows, adding to his look of satirical devilment.

When he bent over to inspect the recalcitrant appliance, she had the strongest urge to reach out and smooth away the bit of dark brown hair that fell over his forehead. He wore his hair short on the sides. She didn't know much about men's hairstyles, but she knew this one tempted her to run her hands through his hair and watch it fall back into place.

But these were all surface things. She was looking for more: for the reason for her attraction to him, for the cause of this magical hum. Because, as Skye had pointed out, Holly had met her share of good-looking men and had rarely been attracted. Oh, she had noticed them. She'd truly enjoyed looking at them. But she'd never felt anywhere near this weak at the knees. So what was it about Rick that got to her so badly?

She deliberately didn't look away when he sent her another teasing look. Instead she looked past that, to the layers beneath the surface flirting. Holly had spent most of her life trusting her instincts. Judging people on the basis of her feelings. It's just that she'd never met a man who was such a dichotomy and for whom her feelings were so complicated.

His attitude made him sexy. But it wasn't an attitude of which she approved. So who could make sense of it? She couldn't. Not logically. But then she'd never been one to base her judgment calls on logic.

She concentrated, refusing to give up until she had this thing figured out. Beneath the flirtatious move of his hand was a surprising gentleness. Touch was important to Holly, probably because she'd had so little of it as a child stuck in a different boarding school every year. She was very sensitive to it. She could pick up on hidden messages. Things like disrespect, slyness, condescension—these she could frequently sense from a person's touch. She sensed none of these in Rick's touch.

Rick interrupted her reflections to ask, "You got a tool chest or a screwdriver around here?"

"Over there." Holly pointed to her carpetbag of tools sitting in the far corner of the room.

"Only you would keep your tools in something like this," Rick commented.

"Only me? What's that supposed to mean?"

"Tools are supposed to be respected. Cared for. Handled with consideration for their value."

Holly wondered if Rick felt that way about women, too. Despite his flirtatious moves, he had treated her with care. He hadn't impatiently tried to yank her dress from the vacuum's hold. He had clearly known what he was doing when he began untangling her skirt from the vacuum's roller jaws.

The long sleeves of his denim shirt were carelessly folded back to his elbow. As he worked, she focused on his arms, which were lightly dusted with hair. Strong arms. Powerful. He'd held her in them. She'd felt their strength. They weren't the arms of a pencil pusher.

"You play baseball as well as watch it?" she suddenly asked him.

"Me?" Rick looked at her with a surprised laugh. "Nah. I'm not a team player. I boxed some when I was in the service."

Her eyes moved to his hands. They were wonderful hands. Long fingers she already knew could be gentle as well as provocative. And he'd risked hurting them in a fight? "Why did you box?"

"Because I was good at it," he said simply.

Once she'd exchanged her image of Rocky for Sugar Ray Leonard, Holly was able to fill in a blank in her notebook on Rick. A boxer had to be light on his feet. That would explain Rick's moves—the confidence of his walk—not to mention the iron tautness of his stomach muscles. He had a seductive self-assurance that was as powerful as any of his physical attributes.

Of course, there were times when he was too damn cocky, but then he was a man and was bound to have flaws, Holly thought on a cheeky note. But despite his sexist attitudes and brash demeanor, Holly sensed that Rick had a tender side, buried deep, deep inside. And she was drawn to that tender side. She sensed it was in there and she wanted to chip away at his macho exterior until she hit that pay dirt.

Because a man who was truly that cynical, analytical and chauvinistic wouldn't have been embarrassed by a three-year-old girl like Asia. And he wouldn't have taken Byron at face value. Guido had told her how Rick had treated Byron as an equal during their poker game. He hadn't been condescending. Byron had been delighted by the fierce competition, claiming that months of fleecing Guido and Whit had left him yearning for a worthy opponent. He'd gotten one in Rick.

And so had Holly.

"You're staring," Rick said.

"I do that sometimes," Holly readily admitted. "When I'm thinking."

"What were you thinking about?"

"That you were lucky you didn't break your neck boxing."

"I was really lucky I didn't break my nose." He ran his index finger down the smooth contour. "I'm kind of proud of that."

"You're proud of the damnedest things."

"So you've already told me."

"And you can just stop giving me that grin."

"What grin?" he countered with devilish innocence.

"That one. The Rhett Butler riverboat gambler's grin."

"No mustache." Rick rubbed the smooth skin between his upper lip and his nose. "Gable had a mustache."

It would be a crime to cover the delicious curve of Rick's upper lip with a mustache, but Holly wasn't about to tell him that. He was enough of a handful as it was. No point in making him even more difficult to handle.

She could have gone on about that glint in his eyes, the one that was part dare, part challenge—duels at dawn, sex at sunrise. But she kept her thoughts to herself, for the same reason. Rick was difficult enough already. She needed to keep what advantages she had, because Holly had a feeling she might need them.

"There you go," Rick said. "You're free."

Yes, she was. And Holly planned on staying that way. "Thanks." She quickly scrambled to her bare feet. "I hate being trapped like that."

"Why? Were you locked in a closet as a kid or something?" Rick meant it as a throwaway comment, a joke.

"I was locked in a number of places in a number of ways," Holly replied, her eyes filled with shadows. "Seems I don't deal well with authority figures."

"That why you don't get along with your dad?"

"Could be."

"Maybe he's changed. Mellowed. Have you thought of that?"

"Nope."

"Maybe you should. Maybe he's different now."

"I sincerely doubt that," she retorted. Frowning at him, she added, "Why are you so keen on reuniting me with my father, anyway? This is the second time you've brought it up."

"Because, like I said before, I know what it feels like to have a parent up and die on you. A lot of things get left unsaid that way. Unfinished."

"I realize that. This situation with my father is not by choice."

Great, Rick thought to himself. Finally he was getting someplace. Pushing the right buttons. "It's not?"

Holly shook her head. "Given a choice, I'd rather get along with him. But given the way he is, I just don't think that's possible."

"You'll never know till you try."

"Trust me, it's not healthy for me to even be in the same room with my father." As far as Holly was concerned, she was pushing it by even being in the same state with him.

She'd stayed away from this part of the country for years. But when things started coming together for Inner View, and this site had become available, she'd known it was time to return. She wasn't going to let her father keep her from doing something she needed to do. She wasn't going to let her inner fear that he'd somehow force her to go back to him stand in her way.

"Don't tell me you're afraid of him," Rick said in disbelief at the emotions he saw flickering across her face.

"In a funny kind of way, I suppose I am afraid of him," Holly reluctantly admitted. "I had to fight so hard to get away from his sphere of influence. It doesn't come naturally to me to break a family tie that way. It's not easy for me to hurt someone. Not that my father would be hurt by anything I did," she added. "That implies a level of emotion that he doesn't possess. I'm sure he was more aggravated by my behavior than hurt."

As Rick well knew, Old Man Redmond was still aggravated.

"He doesn't like losing, you see," Holly continued. "And he feels he lost me . . . as one might lose a possession. And that made him angry. My father is not fun to be around when he's angry. He's not fun to be around, period," she noted with an irreverent grin. "But when he's angry..." Her grin immediately faded and her eyes once more became shaded with bad memories. "It's no picnic, let me put it that way."

"He hit you?"

"Not with his fists. With his words. And verbal abuse can leave scars, just as physical abuse does. I keep telling myself I'm safe here. That it's okay now. And most of the time, I believe it. In fact, ninety-nine-point-nine percent of the time I *do* believe it."

"And the rest of the time?"

"I have nightmares," Holly said simply. She shivered, remembering the familiar form those nightmares took. There were variations, but the central theme was always the same. She was put in a straitjacket and locked in a cage in a room with no windows. And then her father would walk in and throw a black blanket over her and she'd suffocate. She always woke up moaning and gasping for breath.

Rick saw the look on Holly's face, even though he didn't want to. None of this was news Rick wanted to hear. He didn't want to know her innermost fears about her father.

Maybe she was exaggerating the real situation. He knew she had a vivid imagination. Hell, creativity was her specialty. She was sensitive and probably took things too hard, too personally. Women were like that.

But the old macho rhetoric wasn't working its usual magic on Rick's psyche. The thought of someone being knowingly cruel to Holly made his blood boil. He'd felt the same way as a kid with bullies in the neighborhood who'd abused animals. In fact, he'd spent the afternoon at the police station and his father had hit him with a belt after Rick had gotten in trouble for punching a kid who'd tried to set a dog on fire.

But life had knocked those feelings out of Rick. He'd grown up. Learned you couldn't fight the world's battles. It didn't change anything. In the end, you had to look out for yourself... because if you didn't, no one else would.

Looking out for Holly wasn't Rick's job. Getting her back to her father was. He had to keep reminding himself of that fact.

Six

―――――

"So, are you coming to the party tonight?" Byron asked Rick during lunch the next day.

"What party?"

Byron suddenly looked uncomfortable. "Maybe I shouldn't have said anything."

"Too late. You already have. How about filling me in?"

"It's Holly's birthday. We're having a surprise party for her."

"It's Holly's birthday?" Rick repeated. "You're sure?"

"Of course I'm sure. That's a weird question."

Not weird at all, considering the fact that Rick happened to know that Holly's birthday was on Christmas Day. He'd seen her birth certificate. It was in his file on her.

Of course, he couldn't tell Byron that. So he fabricated something. Rick was good at fabrication, also known as scamming. "It's just that we were just talking about birthdays and she didn't mention a word about hers," Rick invented.

"She wouldn't have. She doesn't like anyone to make a fuss. But no way did we get the day wrong," Byron stated. "We always celebrate her birthday on July 22."

Not wanting to get Byron suspicious, Rick just said, "Hey, a surprise party sounds great. Anything I can do to help?"

"Actually, there is. Think you could distract her for a while right after dinner tonight?"

"Sure thing." Distracting Holly was something in which Rick took great pleasure.

"Thanks. That would be great."

Making love to Holly . . . now that *would be great.* Rick's thoughts caught him by surprise. Where the hell were these ideas coming from? It wasn't like him to waste his fantasies on a client's daughter this way.

Rick was supposed to be distracting Holly. Not the other way around. No way. He was in charge, in control. She was the flighty one, not him. Hell, his feet were so firmly planted on the ground they were growing roots!

"So what's the plan? Did they put you in charge of distracting me?" Holly asked Rick when he caught up with her outside of the dining hall.

"I don't know what you're talking about," Rick denied.

"You're an awful liar," she informed him.

If only she knew, Rick thought to himself broodingly. He was an incredibly good liar. He was only an awful liar when he wanted to be.

Mistaking his expression for one of discomfiture, Holly patted his arm reassuringly. "If it makes you feel any better, I already know they're planning a surprise party for my birthday tonight. In about twenty minutes, as a matter of fact."

"What makes you think that?"

"The fact that every July 22 they have a surprise birthday party for me."

Rick wondered how she worked this deal ... celebrating her birthday six months away from the actual date of her birth. Did she opt to stay younger an extra six months? Hell, she was a woman. No doubt about it. He was willing to bet she'd go for the younger age. "How old are you?"

"What kind of question is that?" she demanded.

"An appropriate one to ask you on your birthday."

"How old do you think I am?" she countered.

He knew she was twenty-eight, so he said twenty-six.

Grinning at him, she said, "Close."

"Close?" he repeated. "Which means?"

"Which means I'm close to twenty-six."

"What's this? You're sensitive about your age?"

"I'm not sensitive about my age."

"Then why this runaround?"

"How old are *you?*" she countered.

"Thirty-four," he immediately replied. "And you are?"

"Not answering you. You're thirty-four? Really? I would have guessed you to be older than that."

"This your way of paying me back for asking about your age?"

"Not at all. Tell me, when you were a little kid, what did you want to be when you grew up?"

"Filthy rich."

"And are you?"

"No. But I enjoy what I do."

"A very important element in one's life."

"It doesn't put food on the table, though," Rick noted.

Holly eyed him from head to toe. "You don't look like you've gone hungry."

"Depends what kind of hunger you're referring to," he murmured, his voice a lesson in temptation. "The other night, outside your cabin, I was starving. Absolutely famished.''

She leaned toward him confidingly. "There are things you can do about that, you know. A brisk swim in the lake is quite good. Takes the edge off.''

"That's not all it might take off. That lake is damn cold!''

Holly grinned. "Exactly. Nothing like a good cold swim to take your mind off your hunger.''

"Funny. I can think of any number of things a hundred times better for curing that kind of hunger.''

"I'm sure you can. You see, it isn't that difficult being creative after all, is it? Now, about my birthday party...''

"The one you're not supposed to know you're having.''

Sensing some implied criticism in his comment, she defended herself. "It's at *my* cabin. Why do you think I was using my new vacuum cleaner yesterday?''

"I have no idea.''

"I was getting ready for the party.''

"By nearly committing hara-kiri with the vacuum?''

She ignored his mocking comment. "I even selected the music.''

"Surprisingly efficient of you. I just have one question.''

"Shoot.''

"Why do your friends keep giving you a surprise party when it's obviously no longer a surprise to you?''

"Simple. They don't know I know.''

"They don't?''

"Of course not. That would ruin things for them. They like giving me a surprise party, and I like it as well.''

"But it's not a surprise,'' Rick pointed out with the ultrapatience one used toward two-year-olds.

"I act surprised.''

Not for the first time, Rick wondered how much of the rest of her behavior was an act.

"Why are you so insistent about this subject?" Holly demanded.

"Because it doesn't make any sense to have a surprise party that's not a surprise. It's not logical."

"That's why I like it."

"Figures."

"Come on, let's go." She took him by the hand. "It's time."

The party kicked off, appropriately enough, with the Beatles song "Birthday." From there, Holly had chosen selections as diverse as her tastes—from Motown to New Age, from the Temptations to Enya—with the occasional piece of classical music by Vaughan Williams or Claude Debussy mixed in, as well.

Rick noticed the eclectic collection of music even if he didn't recognize all the individual composers. The last time he'd been in Holly's cabin he'd focused on her. This time he took stock of his surroundings. The furnishings here reflected the same creative ingenuity he'd come to associate with her.

She didn't have a great deal of furniture, and none of it looked like something off the showroom floor, but what pieces she did have were made special with personal touches. A star quilt in shades of rose and blue was carefully placed over the back of the couch. An overstuffed monstrosity of a chair was filled with needlepoint pillows in all shapes and sizes. Rick briefly wondered if Holly had sewn any of them herself. Somehow he couldn't see her sitting still long enough to do so.

Above the natural stone fireplace was a striking poster of a sunrise over the mountains with streaks of brilliant color making the sky look as if it were on fire. There was nothing delicate about it. The poster was as passionate and bold as the woman to whom it belonged.

There were bits of whimsy in every corner: antique baskets with small teddy bears in them, a pewter teapot with a dried flower arrangement in it, a Raggedy Ann doll propped next to a Victorian birdcage with English ivy growing out of it, a large weather-beaten wooden swan with a feather boa around its neck being used as a doorstop.

For someone who was on the move a lot, she sure had managed to collect a lot of stuff, Rick noted. At the moment, she was busy collecting even more stuff as she began opening her gifts.

Her pleasure was equal for the simple paintings given to her by the kids in her class and the obviously expensive Native American jewelry set given to her by Sharon and Charity. What kind of woman liked a kid's scribbles as much as nice jewelry? None that Rick had ever known.

But then Holly was definitely one of a kind, which just meant she was harder to figure out. He had every confidence that he'd succeed in the end, however.

Holly felt Rick's eyes on her. Their brooding intensity was becoming all too familiar to her. She shoved up the sleeves of her long black sweater and smoothed out a fold in her swishy black-and-white printed skirt. This was one of the few black-and-white outfits she owned, but she figured the white anklets with a black dalmatian print and her granny boots prevented it from being too boring. So why was Rick looking at her that way?

Did he think she was too eccentric? Did she care if he did?

"Here, open my present next," Guido said, interrupting her turbulent thoughts.

Holly did so, and found a gorgeous watercolor of a field of wildflowers framed and unusually matted.

"It's beautiful, Guido. Absolutely stunning." Holly gave him a giant hug. "Thanks so much."

"Think nothing of it, kiddo," Guido blushingly replied.

The presents kept coming: a woven cape from Skye, a new teapot from Byron, an assortment of tea and imported biscuits from Whit.

After everything had been opened, Charity helped Holly gather up the wrapping paper. "You've been awfully quiet the past few days, Charity," Holly noted. "You're not still worried about the baby, are you? You said the doctor gave her a clean bill of health. She seems fine." Guido was cooing over the baby at the moment, keeping her occupied while Charity assisted Holly.

"No, I'm not worried about the baby," Charity replied.

"Then what is it?"

Charity sighed. "It's Byron."

"What about him?"

"He's ignoring me again. Haven't you noticed the way he makes a point of being at the opposite end of whatever room I happen to be in?"

"No, I can't say that I have noticed that."

"Well, it's the truth."

Holly could see the silent misery in her friend's eyes. "You really care for him, don't you?"

"You could say that. Sort of the way you care for Rick."

"Rick?" Holly was flabbergasted. "Wait a second here...."

"You've been staring at him all night, Holly. Takes one to know one. I recognize the symptoms."

"He's easy on the eyes, that's all."

"Sure." Charity's tone of voice clearly indicated she wasn't buying that excuse for one second.

"Let's get back to you and Byron...."

"Let's not. It's clear to me that he's not interested. It's no big deal."

"Sure." Now it was Holly's turn to sound disbelieving.

They were interrupted by the arrival of Holly's birthday cake, a huge German chocolate cake Whit had baked, alight

with candles. Someone turned down the lights and everyone started singing "Happy Birthday."

Everyone but Rick, who stood on the outer fringes, silently watching Holly's friends swarm around her as she
made a wish and blew out the candles. The scene gave him
a funny twinge in his chest. For the first time since he could
remember, being an outsider didn't feel comfortable.

Usually it was a role he relished and preferred. Sometimes even insisted upon. But for one brief moment he
wondered what it would be like to be in the inner circle of
friends, to have Holly look at him with such a wealth of
emotion in her eyes.

You're getting old, Dunbar, Rick immediately taunted
himself. Going soft. He needed a distraction.

"How about another game of poker later?" he asked
Byron a few minutes later.

Guido, who was standing nearby, heard him and put in his
two cents' worth. "I still don't feel real comfortable playing with a numbers cruncher," Guido said.

"You play with me and I play the market," Byron pointed
out.

"You're not a numbers cruncher, just a gambler," Guido
retorted.

"A gambler? Not with my rate of return," Byron declared. "I've got a system."

"You really play the stock market?" Rick asked him.

"Sure. How else do you think I can afford these nice
threads I wear, or the customized car—"

"You drive?" Rick exclaimed in surprise.

"Of course I drive."

"But you're—"

"—in a wheelchair. Yeah, I know. I had noticed that,"
Byron said mockingly. "Good thing the car has got hand
controls then, huh?"

Rick felt like an idiot. "I didn't realize . . ."

"A lot of people don't," Byron said quietly. "They look at me and all they see is the *dis*ability. Not my abilities. Not me. I may not be able to do certain things, and I may have to do other things in a different way than I did before the car accident that put me in this wheelchair six years ago, but I've still got the skills that I had before. Developed some new ones, as well. Like playing basketball. If you want to see a mean game, sit in sometime when the guys at the rehab center and I really get going. We take no prisoners."

"I'll keep that in mind," Rick said.

"You do that. And if you want a few tips on the market, let me know. Want any tips in any other department, let me know, too," Byron added with a brief but meaningful look in Holly's direction.

Rick was startled. "You and Holly? You two were—"

"Close friends," Byron inserted. "She's always been like a sister to me, even before the accident."

"You know what's going on between her and her dad?" Rick asked, now that Guido had moved out of hearing range.

"I met the man, used to work for him at one time," Byron replied. "He's not exactly Father of the Year material, if you get my meaning."

"Not many dads are," Rick said.

"Maybe not, but Howard Redmond is in a class all by himself. The guy's a control freak. I don't know if you've noticed, but Holly is something of a free spirit."

"That's putting it mildly," Rick muttered.

"Her father tried to break her spirit while she was growing up. He almost succeeded, too, from what I understand. Holly's much better off away from him."

"You two look deep in conversation over here," Holly noted brightly, having just joined them. "What's so interesting?"

"Byron was just giving me a few tips," Rick said.

"About the stock market? I tell you, he's got a sixth sense about these things," Holly said with admiration. "He handles all my investments for me."

"As long as that's all he handles," Rick muttered under his breath. What was this? He really didn't appreciate the way these thoughts kept sneaking up on him out of nowhere. He should be concentrating on how to convince Holly to return to her dad. A false illness, perhaps? Fear her dad was on his last legs? He had to come up with something.

With that thought firmly in mind and blocking out all others, Rick volunteered for cleanup duty after the party was over. Guido clearly wasn't pleased with his presence.

After being the recipient of yet another glower from across the room where Guido was moving furniture that had been set aside for the crowd of people who'd now left, Rick couldn't resist making a comment to Holly, who was helping him gather up dirty glasses.

"You know, Guido really does look like he should be on *Saturday Night Wrestling*," Rick noted.

"You of all people should know better than to judge a book by its cover. After all, you don't exactly look like an accountant," she reminded him. "The truth is that aside from being a talented artist, Guido is also a successful entrepreneur."

"Yeah, I can just imagine," Rick drawled.

"You're imagining wrong," she informed him tartly. "Guido will be giving a presentation tomorrow for your group about problem-solving."

"That should be interesting."

"I'm sure it will be," she agreed.

"And what exactly are his qualifications for giving this presentation tomorrow?"

"He designed a better mousetrap," Holly replied.

"Meaning what?"

"Meaning he came up with a better mousetrap. Literally. A more humane one that doesn't kill the mouse, just captures it so that it can be released outside. Guido developed it, and it took him ten years to get it marketed. He'll be talking about those experiences when he does his seminar tomorrow."

"You're kidding, right?"

"Absolutely not. In the past, the participants have found Guido's insights to be particularly helpful."

"I'll bet."

"You'll find out for yourself."

So he would. Meanwhile he had to find a way of getting Holly back to Seattle and that five grand into his bank account.

"I didn't give you anything for your birthday," Rick said softly.

"That's okay. You didn't even know it was my birthday until today."

That was certainly true. He only knew it *wasn't* really her birthday. "I do have a little something...."

"You do?"

Rick nodded. Leaning closer he brushed his lips against hers. "Happy birthday, Holly," he whispered, his words creating brushes of whispered delight over her tingling mouth.

It was different from the first time he'd kissed her—softer, more tender—yet her reaction was the same. Intense. Immediate. And disconcertingly intimate. Which was silly. It was over almost before it had begun. Nothing more than a simple birthday kiss. Yet the memory lingered long after he'd left.

Hoping to clear out her jumbled thoughts, Holly stepped outside. She stood on her front porch, her left arm wrapped around the porch column as she leaned against its sturdy support.

The air was fresh with the scent of pine from the surrounding forest. It was a smell that Holly never grew tired of and one that never failed to make her smile. Companies had spent bundles trying to capture that fresh scent, but there was no comparison to the real thing. Even potpourri paled in comparison to the living aroma of the real thing.

Just as other men's kisses paled in comparison to Rick's. She resolutely directed her thoughts elsewhere...to how far they'd come in the past year here at Inner View. They were now averaging forty participants in the weekly business management sessions and the response forms filled out at the end of the program had all been positive so far.

It was only their second year, but the fact that her computer buddy sent the people in his ever-growing computer company in Tacoma to Inner View was a big help, not only during their first year but now as well. Word-of-mouth recommendation had resulted in their currently getting participants from almost a dozen different companies. The money provided by the business management creativity seminars funded the children's programs for those unable to pay.

Holly was pleased with the way things were working out. In this area of her life, anyway. Things with Rick were something else again. She would have liked to think that she had everything under control and that he was coming to see the error of his ways. But she'd never been one to kid herself. Granted she was making some small inroads, but she hadn't won the war by any means. Not yet.

But she wasn't giving up hope. After the vacuum cleaner incident yesterday Holly was as confident as ever that Rick was worth saving, so to speak. She wasn't sure exactly what she was saving him from—his own cynicism, perhaps. From being a loner who thought people were no damn good. From loneliness.

That was what she'd seen in his eyes tonight. Beneath the mockery. Beneath the humor. Loneliness. She'd been there.

Moving from one boarding school to another, never staying long enough to make friends, always feeling out of place and unwanted. Marching to the beat of a different drummer was all very well and good, but it often meant that you walked alone.

Rick was one who walked alone, too. Holly smiled into the darkness as she reflected on the fact that here was yet another thing she and Rick had in common. On the surface, they seemed light years apart, but the more she dug, the more similarities she discovered. And the more intrigued she became.

Intrigued was fine, she told herself. Besotted wasn't. As long as she could tell the difference she'd be fine.

Rick's restlessness didn't improve after another night of intermittent sleep. He still hadn't gotten the damn batteries for his portable radio/cassette player, let alone the burger he'd been craving. By that afternoon Rick knew that if he didn't get away from Inner View, he was going to go nuts.

He told himself it was the aftermath of being around all these artsy-craftsy folks. The poker game with Guido, Whit and Byron the other night had helped, but he needed some heavy-duty *male* stuff—power tools, not cooking tools or management tools. So he called in reinforcements.

Rick had to break down and use the pay phone since the Inner View office was still open and occupied. Also open and semioccupied was the area around the phone, giving him zip privacy. No phone booth, this model just hung from a pole and looked like it had been installed when Eisenhower was still president.

"It's Rick here," he said into the phone.

"Where the hell are you? Are those birds I hear in the background?" Rick's part-time assistant, Vin, demanded.

"Shut up, kid, and listen." Rick's growled comment drew a frown of disapproval from Skye, who was passing nearby. "Uh, sweetheart, it's me."

"Sweetheart?" Vin repeated in shock. "Oh, right. Code, right? You can't talk, so we're talking in code. That was our code sentence, right? I got it now. Hey, this is awesome. We haven't used code all year. So tell me what you want me to do, boss."

"Shut up and listen."

"Is that another code sentence? Hell, boss, I think I shoulda written 'em down somewheres. Or wait a second. Were you talking in code or for real?"

"For real." Jeez, good help was hard to find these days, Rick noted in exasperation. The 22-year-old had come to Rick listing as his job goals starting his own bank...or robbing one. In Rick's opinion, the kid had been into kick-boxing a little too long. There were times, and this was one of them, when Rick wondered if Vin hadn't suffered a little irreversible damage to his frontal lobe.

"I think we should get together," Rick said carefully.

"Sure thing, boss. Just tell me where and when."

"The gas station. In three hours...."

"What gas station?" Vin interrupted.

"Give me a second and I'll tell you. The one in town. There's only one, I'm sure. The place isn't big enough for two," Rick muttered before giving Vin directions.

"I'll be there, boss," Vin promised. "Over and out."

Shaking his head, Rick hung up and then redialed his own number, checking the messages on his answering machine, which he'd been doing daily.

There was an impatient and curt message from Holly's father. "Where the hell are you? And why haven't you called me yet? What's taking so long? Work on her, Dunbar."

Dammit, it had only been a few days. What was the old man's problem? He'd given Rick ten days.

"Something wrong?" Holly asked as he slammed down the pay phone.

"No. Nothing at all," Rick growled, giving her a dirty look before stomping off.

"I wonder what put him in such a snit?" Holly murmured.

"Who?" Skye asked as Holly caught up to her.

"Rick."

"Maybe he had a fight with his girlfriend on the phone," Skye suggested.

"He was talking to his girlfriend on the phone?"

"He was calling someone sweetheart. Could have been his mother, I suppose."

"His mother is dead," Holly stated.

"So is Rick if he's been two-timing you," Skye murmured darkly.

"Skye, you're making too much out of this."

"Out of what?"

"Everything. Rick and I . . . the phone call. . . . He's just one of the participants here, that's all."

"A participant in what, is my question. A little fooling around on the side? Some seduction in his spare time?"

"You make him sound like a gigolo or something," Holly protested.

"How do you know he's not?" Skye countered.

"My instincts."

Skye looked impressed. She knew how on-the-money Holly's instincts were. "I admit, your instincts are rarely wrong. You even ferreted out that insurance con man who was trying to sell us a bill of goods."

"It's a skill I learned at an early age," Holly mockingly noted. "Ferreting out the phonies."

"Still, my instincts are pretty good, too," Skye said. "And there's just something about Rick...."

"There's more there than meets the eye," Holly inserted.

"Yes."

"I agree," Holly said. "There's something he's hiding, but I don't think it's another woman. Not that *I'm* his woman.... What I mean is, he's not shallow. I can see flashes of deep emotion when I look in those dark blue eyes of his. Beneath that infuriating macho exterior I sense ... I don't know ... a heart of gold, maybe."

"How far beneath the exterior?" Skye countered. "Are we talking a few inches or miles here?"

"All right, I'll admit it might take some digging," Holly said. "But you know how I enjoy a challenge."

"Yeah, I know. That can get you into trouble, and has in the past. Like the time you climbed a tree in roller skates because someone dared you to. You ended up breaking your arm and your leg."

"I was only ten at the time," Holly protested.

"Okay. Then how about the time you drove from Chicago to Florida and back in one weekend?

"I made it, didn't I?"

"Barely. The old heap you were driving started on fire just north of Peoria."

"How about the time that they told me I couldn't make a go of a communal fish cannery?" Holly countered. "Or how about that flower farm in Oregon? Or how about using the outer islands for sheep grazing in Maine? Rehabbing the community center on the indian reservation in Arizona? Those were all challenges that I met. For all of that, Inner View is a challenge. Something outsiders thought couldn't be done. They didn't understand the concept at all. Told me I should do something more practical, like open a tourist camp."

"All right, all right. You've made your point. Just be careful," Skye said.

"This from someone who reprimands her two oldest children for being too cautious?" Holly teased her.

"Sherwood and Forest are different. I still can't believe they've chosen to go to Seattle. Sherwood is working in a bank now and Forest is a computer programmer. And what's just as bad, they've changed their names to John and Jim." Skye shook her head in bewilderment. "I don't know where I went wrong as a mother."

"You didn't go wrong. You were and are a special mom. John and Jim . . . I mean, Sherwood and Forest just had to find their own way. That's how you raised them, Skye. To think for themselves. Most moms would be pleased with a banker and a computer programmer in the family. But then you're not most moms, I know that."

"Sherwood was so good at origami."

"There's not much call for that in the job market these days, unfortunately," Holly pointed out.

"And Forest . . . I really thought he was going to go into boat building."

"Computers are a more stable line of work. The most important thing is that they're happy with what they're doing, right?"

"You're right, I know." Skye sighed. "I just feel so cut off from them sometimes. As if they're going to leave us behind and go on with their new life without us."

"You didn't raise them that way, either," Holly pointed out, putting a reassuring arm around her friend. "You taught them the importance of people in their lives. The importance of family."

"That's right. I did teach them that, didn't I? You're right."

"But of course," Holly replied cheekily.

"Besides, no one makes lentil loaf like Whit does. And my Banoffee pie ain't bad, either. You remember the one, with the sweetened condensed milk, coffee and banana? Not that I raised my kids to value material things...other than good food," Skye tacked on.

"Your Banoffee pie is without compare," Holly confirmed. "And so are you, Skye." Holly gave her a big hug. "So are you."

Rick sat in his car, impatiently drumming his fingers along the top of the steering wheel as he waited for Vin. He'd already scouted out their next destination—a seedy-looking bar on the outskirts of town. Like the gas station, it was the only one in town.

"Psst, it's me, boss."

"What are you wearing that getup for?" Rick demanded.

"I thought I was supposed to be undercover or something," Vin replied.

"Wearing a Halloween mask is not going undercover."

"You mean you could still recognize me? I'm supposed to look like Frankenstein."

"For God's sake, take that stupid thing off before they think you're planning on holding up the gas station."

"Gee, I never thought of that."

"That's why I'm the boss and you're not."

"I guess so," Vin said.

"Just get in the car, would you."

"Sure thing." Vin slid into the seat beside Rick. "So where are we going?"

"To a bar. To get a drink."

Vin perked up. "A bar? You paying? I mean, since I'm working and all..."

"I'm paying, Vin."

As Rick suspected from the looks of the place outside, the bar's interior was a mecca for machodom. There were over a dozen dead animal heads mounted over the bar and on the walls. Other parts of the poor animals' anatomy were mounted toward the back of the bar, where he saw a shabby pool table. Guns and knives were also displayed with pride.

There were no fancy hors d'oeuvres on the menu. In fact, no menu. It looked like the only food served was beer nuts, to increase the customers' thirst. No foreign-label beers, either. "I'll take two of whatever you've got on draft," Rick told the bartender, a rotund guy who made Guido look skinny. This was a man's domain. No giggling waitresses here.

When the beers were served Rick put some bills on the bar and handed Vin a glass.

"Let's take a table, so we can talk," Rick said.

"I stopped by and picked up some of your mail, boss," Vin said as they sat down. "And I brought you some of these." Vin handed him a large manilla envelope.

Rick looked inside. Surely he wasn't seeing what he thought he was seeing. Dozens of...

"My mother, she said a man should never be without condoms," Vin explained. "I know you came up here in a hurry, no time to pack some. They probably never even heard of them way up here."

"I didn't come here to screw around," Rick growled. "I came to work."

"I know, boss. But you might get lucky. You never know."

"I don't need any sex education lessons from a kid still wet behind the ears," Rick growled.

"I know that, boss. That's why *I'm* talkin' to you instead."

Rick rolled his eyes and tossed down half his beer in one gulp.

"Don't think I don't appreciate everything you done for me," Vin was saying.

"Everything you *did* for me," Rick automatically corrected him.

"What did I do for you?" Vin repeated, confused. "You mean the condoms...?"

"I meant, the correct English is: What you did for me. Not done for me," Rick impatiently gritted out. "Oh, I give up. Forget it." Who was he to be correcting this kid's grammar? He was hardly in any position to be handing out advice of any kind.

"I don't forget, boss. When no one else would hire me, you did."

"You work cheap," Rick stated.

"You are an amazing man. Truly generous."

"Yeah, that's me. Mr. Generosity."

"You wanna talk about what's bothering you?" Vin asked.

"No. I want another beer. Hey, what's it take to get some service around here?" Rick demanded impatiently.

"Keep your shirt on," the bartender boomed.

"Yeah, keep your shirt on," a tough-looking guy from the next table repeated.

"You two aren't from around here, are you?" the guy's buddy noted. He was big, Rick noticed, and his tattooed biceps were considerable. He got up and walked to Rick's table, towering over Rick and Vin.

"No, I'm not," Rick growled. "You wanna make something of it?"

"What if I did?"

"I suggest you take your tattoos elsewhere if you want them to remain in one piece."

"You talk tough for a wimpy artist."

"Who says I'm an artist?" Rick retorted.

"You're from out there at Inner View, ain't ya? Ya know what they do out there, guys?" the man asked his tipsy buddies. "They worship the devil. Smoke pot. Do drugs. Have orgies."

"Maybe we should go check it out," the rowdiest one of the bunch said with a nasty laugh.

"It's disgustin'," the guy at Rick's table continued. "I've seen that blond come into town and shake her butt, tryin' to tempt good men into joinin' her commune."

Rick leapt up and grabbed the man by his shirt so tightly that the dirty material of the guy's Grateful Dead T-shirt constricted around his thick neck. "I suggest you shut that big mouth of yours, mister."

"You gonna make me?" Rick's adversary taunted.

"Yeah, I am."

It was a draw as to who threw the first punch, but only Rick's hit its target. And then all hell broke loose as the big guy's beer-drinking buddies joined in. The fight was on.

Rick felt the adrenalin surging through his system. This was what he wanted—to let off some steam, get rid of his frustrations. Then he got hit, and suddenly he wondered if this had been such a hot idea. After all, he *was* outnumbered three to one.

"Feel free to jump in here anytime, Vin," Rick said, ducking blows from both sides.

"You sure, boss? I wouldn't wanna interfere or nothin'," Vin said.

"Get over here!" Rick bellowed, narrowly avoiding another punch.

"Yeah, squirt. Get over here," the tattoed guy snarled.

Rick grinned as Vin felled the guy with one well-placed kick.

Ten minutes later it was all over. Rick was still standing, if a little worse for wear. Throwing his arm around Vin's thin shoulders, he said, "Now, that's what I call having a good time."

"Sure thing, boss. Just stop bleeding on me, would ya? You know I've got a weak stomach."

Seven

Rick returned to Inner View feeling much better than when he'd left, despite the fact that he now sported what promised to be a black eye and a cut jaw that refused to stop bleeding, not to mention a pair of bruised knuckles. At least his nose was still unbroken.

"Rick, wait a second," Holly called out from the steps of the Inner View office. "I wanted to talk to you— What happened!" she exclaimed, having just caught sight of his face in the light streaming down from the mercury vapor light posted above the pay phone.

"Nothing happened."

"Then why are you bleeding?"

"I was in a little fight, that's all," Rick said.

Frowning disapprovingly, Holly grabbed a firm hold on Rick's arm and tugged him toward the office she'd just left.

"What do you think you're doing?" he asked, mildly amused by her militant demeanor.

"You obviously need some patching up. Sit down." She shoved a chair at him.

As a matter of principle, he sat on the corner of the desk instead, watching her as she located a first-aid kit. "I need patching up?" he repeated. "You really think so?"

"Yes, I really think so. You could also use a lobotomy," she muttered as she stood in front of him with a pad of gauze and a bottle of antiseptic. "Have you lost your mind?"

"No, and I plan on keeping it that way. Keep your lobotomies to yourself."

"This is serious, Rick." Sitting the way he was, they were at eye level, and Holly made a point of staring at him with no-nonsense directness. "You could have been hurt."

"You just claimed I *was* hurt."

"I mean really hurt. Now sit still and stop moving around."

"Yes, teacher," he said mockingly.

His refusal to take this seriously prompted her to apply the antiseptic to the cut on his cheek with more relish than necessary.

"Ow!" he practically howled, jerking away from her. "That hurts, damn it!"

"Stop being such a baby." She hadn't used *that* much force or antiseptic—she was too much of a softy at heart.

"Anybody ever tell you your bedside manner stinks?" he growled as she started working on his knuckles.

"I haven't had any complaints before," she blithely returned.

"Well, I'm complaining now."

"I heard."

"Ouch!" He glared at her as she finished her ministrations by bandaging the cut on his face with a butterfly bandage. "You're not paying attention."

"I thought you must be a glutton for pain. Why else would you get into a fight?"

"How about to protect your reputation?" The words were out before he could stop them and the minute they were, he cursed his loose tongue.

"Protect my reputation?" Holly repeated, closing the first-aid kit with a decided click. "What are you talking about?"

"Nothing. Forget it."

"I have no intention of forgetting it."

"Let's just say someone said something I took exception to and leave it at that."

"About me? Don't tell me. Let me guess. They said I was strange, right? That we're doing weird things here at Inner View? That I was a hippie? Probably into drugs? Sexual orgies, too."

He appeared to be startled at the accuracy of her portrayal.

"Don't look so surprised," Holly said. "I've heard it all before. From people who have the intelligence of a flea."

"It doesn't bother you?"

"Of course it bothers me. Nobody likes to be thought of as some kind of freak."

"They didn't go quite that far."

"Not here, maybe. But elsewhere..."

"Elsewhere... what?" Rick demanded.

"I've been treated as an outcast," she said quietly. "Being creative means being different. And being different scares some people, the ones with closed minds who prefer everything neatly boxed up with numbing conformity. I broke the cookie-cutter mold and I paid for it."

"What do you mean you paid for it?"

"People say cruel things." She paused remembering the farm town in Illinois where the local people had done everything short of shooting a gun at her to run her out of town. They hadn't wanted an artist colony, filled with what they considered to be a bunch of misfits, in their town. "There are times when I wonder if mankind isn't really the lowest of all life forms, not the highest."

"Now who's sounding cynical?"

"A momentary condition," she retorted with a slow smile. "I get this way every so often when I haven't had enough chocolate."

"Or when you've been hurt enough. And you have been hurt in the past, haven't you?"

"We've all been hurt."

"Yeah, but some feel it more than others."

She was surprised at his astuteness.

"It's like tearing wings off of butterflies to hurt you," he added softly.

"I'm not a helpless butterfly."

"Not helpless, no." Reaching out, Rick touched her hair, gently tangling his fingers in the glorious silken wildness that tumbled around her shoulders. "Definitely beautiful." He brushed his thumb over the curve of her jaw. "And special." With devilish tenderness, he traced the outline of her mouth. "Downright magical."

At that moment Holly did feel helpless. Helpless to resist. Helpless to deny the excitement, the sheer pleasure of his touch. He did make her feel beautiful. Special. And what they shared was indeed magical.

Without taking his eyes from hers, Rick lowered his mouth to her lips and kissed her. It started off sweetly. Softly. Sensually.

Holly leaned closer into the enveloping warmth of his arms. Sliding her arms around his neck, she winnowed her fingers through his hair. She saw the flare of hunger in his eyes before closing her own. Now she could concentrate on her sense of touch and the pleasure of being touched.

Rick's position, perched as he was on the corner of the desk, added an immediate and provocative intimacy to their embrace. She stood sandwiched between his splayed legs, pressed snugly against the placket of his jeans and the throbbing hardness of his arousal.

Cupping his hands around the curve of her derriere, Rick braced his feet on the floor and lifted her against him. Growling husky words of pleasure, he deepened their kiss with an ardent fierceness that Holly welcomed.

She matched him tongue thrust to tongue thrust. Through the thin stretch material of her turquoise leggings, she could feel the purposeful warmth of his hands behind her and the firm tautness of his need in front of her. With a ragged groan, Rick gathered her even closer. The thrusting imprint of his body left her in no doubt about the hunger she'd aroused in him.

Lifting his mouth from hers, he whispered her name. "Holly."

She shifted against him, almost making him explode.

"Oh, God . . ."

The tortured sound of his voice made her open her eyes. She didn't even know she had her fingers in the back pockets of his jeans until that moment. She'd only known she wanted to get closer, to cure this endless ache deep within her.

"I think we should—"

"Don't think," he interrupted her, his lips feathering across the pulse beating at the base of her throat. "Just feel."

Holly's breath caught in her throat as his hand daringly lowered to cup one of her breasts. He held its burgeoning fullness in the palm of his hand while his thumb traced imaginary paths across the soft slope. Even through the cotton of her oversize T-shirt, the results of his caress were ravishing.

The brush of his fingers created a fire storm of provocative cravings as he caressed the sides of her breasts. She was dying to have him do more than just tease her with his touch. As if reading her thoughts, Rick slipped his hands under her T-shirt and, with the gentle stealth of a pirate, he undid the clasp on her bra. Now his hands were free to stroke the creamy smoothness of her breast without any barriers.

Moving swiftly, he cleared the desk with one arm while lowering her onto its surface with his other arm. Seconds later, Holly found herself stretched out beneath him as if she were the feast at a banquet.

That imagery stayed with her as Rick tugged her T-shirt and loose bra completely out of his way and proceeded to nibble at her with erotic love bites. He aroused her, teased her, soothed her with his tongue. When his lips finally closed around one rosy crest, she almost cried out from the intense pleasure of his mouth surrounding her, tugging on her softly and oh so wickedly.

Holly was lost in a haze of fiery sensations. The need to have him, to take him in her hands and guide him to her was almost overwhelming. She was at the mercy of the desire glowing deep within her, completely overwhelmed by the raging fire of passion.

Her restless wriggling caused her to scoot over the smooth surface of the desk until she was at the edge, both literally and figuratively. Lifting her arms, she threaded her fingers through his dark hair and held him to her. But when she bent her knees to cradle him against her, she felt herself falling—right off the desk!

Rick caught her before she got very far. But the incident was jarring enough to break off their embrace.

Holly couldn't help it. She cracked up. "Had many women fall at your feet this way, Rick?" she inquired with a grin meant to hide the fact that she felt awkward and foolish for being so clutzy.

"You're the first."

His voice was quiet and husky, filled with meanings she couldn't decipher. Things were happening too quickly here, Holly reminded herself. Even for her. Feeling self-conscious, she hurriedly scooted away from him and stood up, smoothing her clothing back into place and praying she didn't look as embarrassed as she felt.

"I'm sorry," Rick said. "Things got out of hand."

"You could say that."

"We're pretty explosive together," he murmured huskily. "I didn't plan on this happening."

"Neither did I," she muttered, keeping her arms tightly wrapped around her middle to prevent her unfettered breasts from jiggling. After all, her bra was still undone. Doing it back up required a contortionist act she wasn't willing to attempt in his presence.

Seeing her predicament, Rick matter-of-factly turned her around and refastened her bra before she could voice a protest. "Thanks," she murmured with a shyness she hadn't felt since she was twelve.

"Thanks for patching me up," he said.

"Sure."

Leaning closer, he kissed her. Just once. It was over almost as soon as it began. . . .

But the memory remained long into the night as Holly restlessly tossed alone in her bed. So much for her teaching him a lesson, she thought to herself as she punched her pillow. It looked like she'd been the one who'd gotten an education—in seduction and raw passion. These were subjects she hadn't explored before and Rick made her want to study them, and him, in infinitely—intimately—closer detail.

* * *

"Hey, mister, were you trying to cut your ear off like that Vincent guy did?" one of Holly's students asked Rick the next day, after Rick finished his morning seminar. Rick frowned trying to think of the kid's name. Bobby.

"What are you talking about?" Rick retorted.

"That bandage on your face. So, were you trying to cut your ear off like that Vincent guy?"

"No." Rick had no idea who this Vincent guy was supposed to be.

"Good. 'Cause you missed. What were you trying to do?"

"Get rid of some frustration," Rick muttered to himself.

Unfortunately, the kid apparently heard him. "So you cut yourself?"

"No. I got sucker-punched."

"Someone punched you?" Bobby was just about dancing around in excitement "Wow! When? Who did it? Did you sock him back? Is he bloody, too? Was there lots and lots of blood?"

"Not a lot of blood, no."

"No." Bobby looked disappointed. "Why not?"

Rick was at a loss here. Granted this kid didn't scare him the way that big-mouthed little redheaded girl did, but still he was no expert with kids. Hell, he had zip experience in this department.

Sure he'd been a kid once, but that had been light years ago. What was he supposed to say? How was he supposed to answer a question like that?

"Hey, you got stars on your bandages!" Bobby noted in admiration, changing the subject much to Rick's relief. "Holly only gives out the star Band-Aids to special people."

Rick looked down at the adhesive bandage circling the knuckle on his index finger. He hadn't even noticed that there was a print on it, but then that wasn't surprising considering his state of mind since he'd almost made love to Holly last night. On a desk. At the Inner View office. He hadn't been that carried away in a long, long time.

His mind was still all over the map, his hormones on overdrive, his arousal on a constant state of alert. It wasn't a comfortable feeling. If he was feeling this restless, he sure as hell hoped that Holly was suffering from the same problem.

"Hey, Holly!" Bobby cried out. "This guy was in a fight."

"So I've heard," Holly replied, joining them.

"You gave him a star Band-Aid," Bobby said.

"We were all out of the regular ones," Holly maintained. "Are you ready to go, Bobby?"

"Sure."

"Where are you going?" Rick demanded, not pleased with the way she was ignoring him.

"To Paradise," Holly answered.

"Paradise, huh?" Rick murmured reflectively. "I thought that's where we were last night."

For once, Holly was at a loss as to how to respond to his seductive comment. No snappy retort came to mind. Instead she remembered the feel of his lips on her breast, and her heartbeat immediately quickened with excitement.

"Mount Rainier," she said, tugging her T-shirt away from her body, which had suddenly gotten very, very warm. "Uh, we're going to Mount Rainier."

"You seem a little distracted, Holly," Rick noted in amusement, pleased that he wasn't the only one affected by what had happened between them last night.

"Do I? It's been a busy night...I mean morning. A busy morning. So, Bobby, you ready to go?"

"Sure."

"This outing for kids only?" Rick inquired.

"No. It's for anyone who wants to come . . . I mean to go. . . ." Holly was practically stumbling over her tongue. "All right, Rick. Stop that!"

"I'm not doing a thing," he maintained, trying to keep a straight face at her flustered expression. "You're the one falling all over yourself."

"Because you're giving me those looks again. Don't deny it."

"You're giving me those looks right back," he countered.

"I guess I am," she admitted with a wry smile. "Okay, what do you say we call a truce?"

"I wasn't aware that we were at war."

"We weren't. We aren't. So are you staying or are you going with us?"

"Oh, I'm *coming,* Holly. Make no mistake about that."

And so Rick found himself in a van with eight other people singing "Ninety-Nine Bottles of Beer on the Wall." He should have driven by himself. He wished he had.

He wasn't the group kind. He was a loner. Groups made him feel like an outsider. They always had in the past. But he noticed a subtle change now. Not enough to make him join in the off-key chorus, but enough to make him relax a bit. Or relax as much as he could, given the fact that Holly was sitting next to him, her denim-clad thigh pressed against his.

She was wearing a surprisingly normal outfit: jeans that were actually blue if well-faded and broken-in to perfection, a white T-shirt with a denim long-sleeved shirt over it and a pair of sturdy hiking boots.

Feeling Rick's gaze on her yet again, Holly started talking. He really was the only man she'd ever met who had this uncanny ability to make her feel nervous and exhilarated all at once. She wasn't sure she was pleased about that, not that there was a damn thing she could do to change it. She knew herself well enough to accept her emotions the way they were, sort of the way she accepted her hair the way it was. Any attempt to restrain it always ended in disaster. She smiled, remembering the way her mother had patiently brushed her hair for her when Holly had been a little girl.

"You know, my mother really loved this mountain," Holly reflected, her voice soft with memories. "She used to tell me that she admired its independence. The way it stands alone, rising above the surrounding foothills."

"I can see it from my place in Seattle," Rick admitted. "On a clear day." If he leaned way out of his small window and looked around the building across the street.

"It's visible from almost every major city in the state. On a dare, a friend of mine and I drove around the state checking out that claim. One night, we ended up sleeping in a bumper car because it started to rain and there was nowhere dry to pitch our tent. We came across this fairground out in the middle of no place."

"This friend of yours a guy?" Rick casually inquired.

"No. She was a girl I met while working one summer at Yosemite National Park. We were both waitressing at the hotel there. I also did some subbing as a tour guide. Wanna hear my sample 'tour voice'?" she asked him with a saucy grin.

Rick nodded.

"Okay, here goes. Listen up, the rest of you guys," she added for everyone else's benefit before making a production of clearing her throat. "Okay, here goes.... Stunning Mount Rainier rises two miles above the surrounding foothills of the Cascades and is one of the great fire peaks of the Northwest." She deliberately packed her voice with plenty of pizazz. "The Indians named this snowy mountain Tacoma. And it *is* snowy there—the greatest snowfall ever recorded anywhere in the world was over ninety-three feet, and it was recorded at Paradise ranger station.''

Holly had to pause a moment to draw in a breath. "Each year, over seven thousand climbers attempt the trek up Mount Rainier. About half of them turn back before ever reaching the top. It's an awesome mountain and a wide one with a circumference at its base of more than one hundred miles!'' she said with dramatic emphasis.

''What's circum—circumcision mean?'' Bobby demanded.

Holly gave Rick a dirty look for cracking up. "Circumference, Bobby. And it means the distance around a circle.''

''I think the mountain looks like the letter *M* with snow on it,'' Jordan stated.

''It looks like my ice-cream cone after I've taken a bite out of it,'' Martha shyly inserted.

''It does look that way,'' Holly agreed.

''Do they have ice cream there?'' Jordan eagerly demanded.

''We'll see when we get there,'' Holly replied.

As it turned out, they did stop for ice cream at the Old Paradise Lodge. The total number in their party turned out to be almost thirty, what with business seminar participants and kids, and it had taken four vans to get them there. Skye and Whit took the kids on a walk along the paved pathway while Holly took a break and sat down on a bench near the lodge to savor the view and her ice-cream cone.

''Nice earrings,'' Rick noted, touching them with his finger and setting them gently swaying before sitting down next to her.

''I got them for my birthday yesterday,'' Holly said in that all too familiar breathless tone of voice she only used when he got too close.

"Yeah, I noticed."

She wondered what else he noticed. Far better to keep his attention on something prosaic like her jewelry. "Do you know what these are?" she asked, touching the earring he'd just touched.

"Sure I know what they are. They're earrings. I might not notice much, but give me some credit."

"I meant the kind of earrings."

"Haven't got a clue. I never claimed to be an expert in women's jewelry."

Just in women, Holly thought to herself. Aloud she said, "They're Dream Catchers."

He squinted. "They look like spiderwebs with feathers attached to them."

"The story of the Dream Catcher is one of my favorites. I think it originated with the Oneida Indians in the northeastern part of the United States. Anyway, the story goes that the Dream Catcher would filter all dreams and let only the good dreams flow through the open circle. They were placed above a baby's cradle to protect them and were kept throughout life."

"Think they'll protect you from nightmares?"

"I can always hope...."

Rick remembered well her comment of the other day...that ninety-nine-point-nine percent of the time she thought she was safe from her father's sphere of influence. And the rest of the time she had nightmares.

He'd been having a few himself. Time was quickly running out here and he didn't know what to do about it. Hell, he didn't even know which way was up anymore. Holly had that effect on him. She had that effect on everyone she came in contact with. Changed them. Made them think.

Much as he hated to admit it, Rick was not only drawn to Holly's enthusiasm and idealism, he could feel a bit of it rubbing off on him, appealing to a part of him he'd thought had died long ago. He'd seen the good she'd done with the kids. The shy little girl he'd noticed in her class a few days ago had blossomed under Holly's enthusiastic attention. Hell, all the kids adored her.

But Rick was no kid. Even so, Holly made him start thinking about the possibilities in life instead of the inequities. Not that there was any possibility of his having an affair with her, damn tempting though it might be.

Aside from it being a bad business practice, Rick told himself he wasn't in the market for any kind of commitment right now. And free spirit though she might be, Holly wasn't the sort of woman for one-night stands. Her romantic history confirmed that.

No, it was an impossibility. But that didn't stop Rick from reaching out to wipe the slight smear of chocolate ice cream from her chin.

"Oops, was I dripping?" she asked, delicately licking her lips in a seductively feline movement. "Is it all gone?"

"No." Rick's voice was gritty with need. Whatever he felt for her, it hadn't been satisfied by their embrace last night. That brief taste of her had only heightened his appetite.

"No?" She turned her face to him. "Where else do I have ice cream on me?"

"Here." He swiped his finger across the right side of her cheek. A small dab of cold ice cream perched on his fingertip. Slowly, deliberately, not taking his eyes from hers, he brought his finger to his mouth.

It was a simple gesture, over in a matter of seconds, yet its effect on Holly was surprisingly strong. She felt all hot and bothered deep inside. Like she was running a fever. Like she was being drawn in . . .

"You guys aren't going to do something gross like kiss, are you?" Jordan demanded.

Holly sprang back guiltily, almost dumping what little was left of her ice-cream cone on her lap. "What are you doing here, Jordan?"

"Looking for the bathroom."

"Jordan, I told you to wait for me," Whit said as he joined them. "Come on, Jordan, the bathroom is this way."

The two left as suddenly as they'd appeared.

Holly's eyes met Rick's. He had a way of transferring his thoughts without saying a word. . . .

She tried to be analytical, telling herself she was relieved to see that the swelling around his eye seemed to have gone down and that it hadn't developed into a full-fledged shiner. She kept getting caught up in the mysterious dark blue depths of his eyes, however, and it took a conscious effort for her to look away from the magnetic draw of his gaze.

"So . . . what do you think of it up here at Paradise?" she asked him.

"It's okay."

"Okay?" Holly stared at him, aghast. *"Okay?"*

"You've got something against okay?"

"To describe this view, yes."

"How would you describe it?"

"Breathtaking. Stunning. Unforgettable. Look out there." She waved her hand. "What do you see?"

"I see a mountain with snow on it."

"That snow happens to be the largest glacial system in the continental United States."

"Now who's being analytical?" he countered.

She ignored his mocking comment. "What else do you see?"

"Pine trees and grass."

"Grass?" She rolled her eyes in dismay. "That's a meadow. Carpeted with wildflowers."

"Carpeted, huh?"

"That's right. This area is famous for its wildflowers this time of year. Look closely, can't you see all the colors? White, pink, purple, yellow... That meadow is like an incredible tapestry woven with blue lupine, magenta paintbrush and yellow monkey flowers."

Rick caught himself smiling at her enthusiasm. "You're one of a kind, aren't you."

"So are you. Grass." She shook her head. "Aren't you ever impressed?"

She impressed him. The way she embraced life with such abandon. But he wasn't about to say that out loud.

"What are you thinking about?" she asked him.

"That liver pâté you had at your party the other night," he said, instead of telling her the truth. "I thought you didn't eat meat."

"I don't eat anything that has a face."

"I guess that means you won't be nibbling on me."

"Guess it does," she agreed.

"Pity."

"Mmm, we all have to make sacrifices. By the way, it wasn't liver pâté. It was nut pâté."

"Get out of here."

"I'm not kidding. It was nut pâté. Whit makes it. Want the recipe? You throw walnuts or pecans into a food processor with a carrot, onion, some bread crumbs, tomato sauce, vegetable bouillon and a little garlic. Pour it into a greased loaf pan and bake it."

"I don't want the recipe," Rick stated emphatically.

"Why not?"

"For one thing, I don't cook. And I don't like nuts."

"You ate the pâté, didn't you? Liked it, too, right?"

"Only because I didn't know there were nuts in it."

"Now who's not being logical?"

"You must be rubbing off on me."

She had to laugh at the accusatory tone of his voice. "I told you we'd change your way of thinking."

"What if I don't want my way of thinking changed? What if I liked it just fine the way it was?"

"You're sounding panic-stricken again, Rick."

"I do not get panic-stricken," he growled.

"Even when little girls mention their unmentionables to you?"

"That kid has a big mouth."

"She likes you," Holly said.

"Give me a break."

"She does. She told me so the other day. Told me she likes the man who runs away from her."

"I do not run. Avoid, maybe. Not run."

"She still likes you."

"Yeah, well, you always chase what you can't have."

"You speaking from experience here?" Holly asked him.

"Maybe. What's that kid's name again? Asia? What kind of person names their kid after a continent, anyway?" Rick irritably demanded.

"You're getting tense again," Holly calmly replied. "You need to sit back and let the healing powers of the mountain steal over you. A friend of mine believes that mountains are a source of natural power and rejuvenation."

"A friend of yours *would,*" Rick retorted.

"You don't believe in much, do you?"

"No."

"That's a shame."

"You believe too much," he said.

"Compared to you, maybe. But compared to all there is to believe in . . . I'm just getting started."

"God forbid. If you're only getting started, we're all in big trouble." Him in particular, Rick silently noted. Because much as he wanted to deny it, Rick had this uneasy feeling he was in danger of getting in over his head with Holly here.

Latest score: fancy lady, three; private investigator, zero in the bottom of the sixth inning. Yep, Rick was definitely beginning to worry.

Eight

When Rick returned to Inner View, he had to check in with his answering machine again from the pay phone. Old Man Redmond had left another message—brief and to the point. "Your time is running out, Dunbar," he warned.

"Tell me something I don't already know," Rick muttered, slamming down the phone.

By the time he arrived at the dining hall, most of the others had finished eating and cleared out. Great. Rick's irritation grew another notch higher. He was already aggravated that Holly had gotten to him today, affecting him. He didn't like his priorities and thought processes screwed up by a sensitive, creative, wild, one-of-a-kind woman.

But what if what she'd told him about her father hadn't been an exaggeration, but the truth? Could he really bring himself to haul her back to that kind of life?

"Hey, Rick! You looking for some dinner?" Whit asked him.

Rick was looking for answers, but dinner would do, so he nodded.

"Sit down," Whit told him. "I saved something special for you."

Rick expected that "something special" to be another vegetarian concoction, made of pureed legumes—or even worse, the dreaded tofu. Much to his surprise, it turned out to be a big, juicy, broiled-to-perfection burger. An answer to a prayer—well, one of his prayers, Rick amended.

"Whit, you are a pal," Rick said eagerly picking up the burger with both hands.

"Don't mention it," Whit replied. "Especially not to Holly."

Rick took a deep breath, savoring the burger's aroma. He was just about to take the first, delicious bite when he noticed an adolescent girl staring at him disapprovingly.

"You do realize that's a corpse you're eating, don't you?" she asked him.

"Is she one of yours?" Rick called out to Skye, who was wiping tables nearby. She nodded proudly. "Figures," he muttered.

"Think about it," the girl said with a shudder. "Corpses."

"I don't have to think about it, kid. I like corpses. Medium rare."

"My name's not kid. It's India."

"Figures," he repeated. First Asia, now India. Could Antarctica be far behind?

"You're not very friendly, are you?" India noted.

"You noticed. Good."

"I *like* people who aren't friendly," India declared. "They're more of a challenge, know what I mean? Holly told me that."

"She would."

"Don't you like Holly? Everybody likes her."

"Yeah, she's a real saint," Rick retorted mockingly. He didn't want to talk about Holly. He didn't want to even think about her right now. He was in no financial position to be choosy about this case. He had bills to pay. He couldn't really afford to walk away from this job, tempting though it might be at times. None of this put him in a good mood.

"Were you born mean or did you become that way later?" India asked with disingenuous curiosity.

Rick frowned at her. "Didn't your mother teach you any manners?"

"Sure she did. I always say please and thank you. And I never lie. Do you lie?"

"Everybody lies." Rick shifted uncomfortably. "Don't you have something else to do besides bothering me?"

"Nope," India said cheerfully. "I've seen you walking around at night. Can't you sleep?"

"It's too damn quiet here. Most of the time. When kids like you aren't badgering me over my dinner." He gave her his best glare.

To his complete surprise, India started blinking furiously, her eyes teary.

"Hey, you're not gonna cry, are you, kid?" Rick demanded. "Tell me you're not gonna cry. Ah, jeez . . ." He swore softly, once, under his breath. "Look, India, I'm sorry, okay? Come on, kid. Take pity on an old guy. I haven't had a burger in almost a week. All I want to do is eat this without comments from the peanut gallery. Okay?" To his relief, India's imminent tears dried up.

"What's a peanut gallery?" India asked.

"Never mind. Before your time."

The kid must have seen his look of frustration because she finally did as he'd asked and took pity on him. "I suppose

I should be polite and let you eat your corpse in peace," she said.

"Thanks a lot," Rick retorted dryly. In peace. That would be the day. He hadn't had any of that since he'd come to Inner View.

Rick's time at Inner View was quickly coming to an end. On his last scheduled day he he woke late and then hurried to a session Byron taught called Expressions in Clay.

He'd spent another restless night last night, only this time it hadn't been the damn trees keeping him awake. It had been Holly. And the memory of her smile, of her mouth on his, of her body pressed so closely against his. . . .

Rick smashed down the clay figure he was working on. His expression at that moment—total frustration. Of all the stuff he'd had to do at Inner View, this art stuff was the hardest for him.

During the past week, Rick had tried his hand at everything from watercolor painting with Guido, which had been a total washout, to weaving with Skye, where he'd been more interested in how the loom worked than how the final product looked. The least irritating of all the things he'd been required to do had been the sessions with Byron, who threw a mean pot, as well as managing an ever-growing stock portfolio.

In the beginning, Rick had stared at the lump of clay for fifteen minutes, not knowing what the hell to do with it, but wanting to toss it against the nearest wall. Apparently sensing his frustration, Byron had suggested that Rick try and create something he felt he could relate to. So in that first class, Rick had chosen a sports car as his subject and had been rather amazed to find that it actually turned out to look like a car.

Today, however, his thoughts were elsewhere. He wondered if he would have to sign up for another week to get his job accomplished.

He was so deep in thought, he didn't realize Byron had joined him until he heard his voice. "Hey, Rick. Nice bust."

"What?!"

"The piece you're working on. It's a woman, right? A sculptured head and shoulders is called a bust."

"Right. I knew that."

"Who is it?" Byron asked.

"I don't know. It's nobody."

"It's good," Byron said. "Kind of looks like Holly, but I'm sure that's *just* a coincidence." With a man-to-man grin, Byron moved his wheelchair to the next participant.

Rick glared at the clay figure. It *did* look like Holly. How had that happened? He'd been thinking about the case and next thing he knew . . . presto.

"So, Rick, how's it going?" Holly said, startling Rick.

First Byron was able to sneak up on him, and now Holly. Talk about his well-honed reflexes falling down on the job. Rick was totally disgusted with himself. "Fine," he growled. "It's going just fine."

"What are you making?" She tried to glance over his shoulder.

Rick immediately returned the clay to its former natural state—a nonidentifiable lump. Not a bust, although he could feel Holly's breasts brushing his shoulder as she inhaled. "Nothing. It's nothing," he said.

Holly could tell that Rick was clearly uncomfortable with her presence. "I'll let you get back to nothing, then. Hey, Byron," she called out. "Okay if I use the potter's wheel in the back?"

"Sure thing, Holly. Go ahead."

"Thanks."

Rick didn't get anything done during the remaining twenty minutes of the class. Holly was nearby, and he was aware of that fact with every fibre of his being. Every throbbing, aching, damn fibre.

It was time to get his mind back on work here. His bills weren't going to pay themselves. He had a job to do. Getting to Holly. Not having her get to him.

"Tell me again how playing with clay is supposed to make me a better manager," Rick said as he joined her in the back after class.

"Because you have to look at things and really notice them in order to reproduce them—in clay or by drawing or painting them."

Rick stood there, watching her fingers curve around the damp clay, forming it, shaping it. The way he wanted to shape her soft breasts, curve her lush thighs.... Damn! It was happening again. He was getting distracted. Time he did some distracting of his own.

"So, how good are you at this?" he asked her, moving closer.

"At what?" she replied, quickly glancing at him over her shoulder.

"Making pots."

"Making pots or making whoopee? You think I don't recognize that gleam in your eye?" she said.

"Mah rivahboat gamblah's gleam?" he asked à la Rhett Butler.

"That's the one. And to answer your question, I'm not very good at this," she said as the bowl she was making fell in on itself. "I've never quite gotten the hang of it, although Byron has tried to show me—"

"Let me try." Rick didn't give her the chance to refuse. Instead he pulled up a nearby stool and placed it right behind her. "You curve your hands around the clay like this, gently." He threaded his fingers through hers, intricately joining them into one entity that was melded together by the dampness of water and wet clay. "That's better...." He slid his slick fingers between hers, tantalizing the delicate web of skin between each digit. His chin rested on her shoulder as he softly murmured, "It'll do whatever you want it to, if you don't push it too far. Or so I've heard."

All Holly could hear was the pounding of her heart. Rick's arms were a ring of fire around her. The sound of his breathing was a constant temptation in her ear. As if that weren't enough, he shifted his thumbs so that they were atop hers and then he ran them from her thumbnail up to the pulse throbbing at her inner wrist.

She leaned back against his chest, fitting herself into the inner contour of his legs, her head thrown back as he nibbled at her neck. She'd pinned her hair on top of her head before using the wheel to keep it out of her way. The hairstyle opened new territory to Rick's adventurous kisses.

That magical telltale hum was there again, singing in her bloodstream, resonating through her entire body. She knew there was some reason they shouldn't be doing this there, but she couldn't for the life of her think what it was at the moment.

She turned her head farther, allowing his lips to get closer to the parted warmth of her mouth.

"So how are things going back here?" Byron asked as he wheeled into the room. "Oh, I see things are going real well, huh?"

"Byron!" Holly almost fell off her stool in her effort to extricate herself from Rick's embrace.

"He already saw us. Too late, Holly," Rick murmured before letting her go.

Holly had the feeling it was indeed too late, too late to tell herself that she was going to teach Rick a lesson and come out of the experience gloriously unscathed. Too late to believe it.

* * *

"So how do you think Rick has done this past week?" Holly asked Sharon as the two of them stood outside the front of the dining hall after lunch that afternoon. "I haven't had the chance to ask you before."

"How has he done? Well, I must admit he was an unwilling participant at first. Didn't seem real impressed or interested in what I had to say. But he did come up with some unusual suggestions in our brainstorming sessions. I think Byron was able to work better with him than I was," Sharon replied.

"Some male bonding thing, no doubt," Holly muttered, still upset over the way she'd responded to Rick earlier that morning, when Byron had caught them necking in the back room.

"Rick has a lot of preconceived ideas about things," Sharon was saying. "That makes it harder to reach him. He doesn't appear to be real open about some things. He has some *very* traditional views. As you know, conformity and creativity are to a large extent incompatible."

"You're saying Rick is a conformist?"

"You don't think so?"

"I suspect he's kind of devious about that. Makes you think he's one thing when he's something else. He makes you think he's this hard-hearted, analytical tough guy...when really he's..."

"Yes...?" Sharon mockingly prompted her.

"Not."

"Not hard-hearted? Or not analytical?"

"There's more to him than meets the eye."

"He certainly can be charming. And he's quick."

"Very quick," Holly concurred with an inner grin. Awkward as it had been getting caught red-handed by Byron, there was no denying the magic of Rick's touch.

Apparently Holly's inner emotions showed in her outward expression because Sharon said, "What's that look for? Are you and Rick . . . ?"

Before Holly could reply, they were interrupted by Asia, who was insistently tugging on the bottom hem of Holly's magenta tunic top. "I gotta va—"

"Is that a new toy you have there?" Sharon hurriedly interrupted, pointing to the brightly colored ball Asia held in her chubby little arms. "It's lovely with all those stars on it."

Asia nodded her agreement. "Pretty ball. Bye now," she said cheerfully.

"Bye now," Holly repeated.

"Call me old fashioned but I still have a hard time with her using the proper terminology like that," Sharon stated as Asia toddled off.

"You and Rick both," Holly replied.

"Holly, don't tell me Asia said that in front of one of the participants! You promised me that you'd talk to Skye about keeping Asia away from the business management people, making sure Asia didn't brag about her personal parts to them."

"I did talk to Skye . . ." Holly paused at the noise of a delivery truck backing up toward the rear entrance of the dining hall. Out of the corner of her eye, she saw Asia chasing her ball, blissfully unaware of the truck about to cross her path.

Rick hung up the pay phone. It wasn't a call he'd really wanted to make, but one he'd had to. He looked up from his position at the pay phone just in time to see Holly dashing directly into the path of a backward-moving truck!

He was too far away to do anything but stand there, his heart in his throat, as Holly grabbed the big-mouthed little girl around the middle and kept running. The truck came so close that Rick could have sworn it touched the swirl of

Holly's skirt. Then his view was blocked by the truck itself. Had it hit her?

He'd never run as fast in his life as he did in that moment. He hadn't prayed since his mother died. But Rick prayed as he raced around the front of the truck. *Let her be all right. Please, God, let her be all right.*

Rick didn't realize he'd held his breath until he saw her, leaning against a tree, but standing upright. He exhaled sharply, his heart a painful spike in his chest.

"Of all the asinine things to do!" he yelled at her.

Holly looked up to see Rick glaring at her.

"What were you trying to do?" he demanded. "Get yourself killed?"

"No." Holly handed Asia over to a trembling Skye. "You better take her inside," she told Skye.

Skye just nodded.

"Are you crazy?" Rick demanded, his voice only a few decibels lower than a jet engine or a rock concert.

"There's no need to yell," Holly retorted mildly. "I think I'm gonna sit down now," she added as her knees started shaking uncontrollably.

Rick was there before she could move an inch, sweeping her up in his arms and holding her as if he'd never let go. "Are you hurt?" His voice had changed dramatically and was now filled with anxiety instead of anger.

"I'm just a little shaken up, that's all."

"You're lucky to be alive," he growled as he carried her the short distance to her cabin.

"Yeah, I guess I'm only just realizing that now."

"What the hell were you thinking of?"

"Saving Asia. She was playing with her ball and not paying any attention to that truck. It was headed right for her and would have hit her."

"It could have hit you, too. Did you stop to think of that?"

"No. There wasn't time to stop and think. Only to act. You would have done the same thing, Rick."

"No, I wouldn't have."

"Yes, you would have," she stubbornly maintained. "And don't give me any of that cynical crap."

"I see almost getting killed has made you even feistier than usual."

"You would not have stood there and done nothing," Holly said.

"What do you think I am? A knight in shining armor to ride to the rescue?"

"You rescued me from landing on my fanny," Holly pointed out.

"You deserve a good swat on your fanny for scaring me that way," he retorted.

Seeing the paleness still lingering around his mouth, she didn't protest his comment. When they reached her cabin, he pushed the unlocked door open with his foot and neatly kicked it closed once they were inside.

"How do you feel?" he asked as he set her down.

"A little shook up. I think it's just nerves—a delayed reaction, I guess. Maybe I should take a hot shower to relax."

"Are you sure you won't fall in the shower?"

"My bathtub isn't really big enough to fall over in. Neither is the bathroom."

"All the same, I'll wait here until you get out. And leave the bathroom door unlocked, just in case something happens," he called after her as she headed for the bathroom.

"Promise not to peek?" she said.

"Scout's honor."

"Were you a Boy Scout?" she asked, stopping at the door.

"No."

"That doesn't change the fact that I still think you would have done the same thing I did, Rick, had our positions been reversed."

After she'd closed the door, Rick muttered, "Then you've got more faith in me than I've got in myself."

Delayed reaction was catching up with him, as well. Rick sank onto the couch. Holding his hand out, he realized it was shaking.

He didn't try to make any excuses for his reaction. The truth was staring him in the face. The truth was taking a shower in the other room.

When he'd seen Holly in danger, all his slick explanations had been stripped away and he'd been hit by the depth of his feeling for her as surely as she'd almost been hit by that delivery truck. This was more than just physical attraction at work here. He cared about her, more fool he.

She didn't linger in the shower. Before he was ready to face her, she was back, standing in the doorway again.

Holly saw the raw emotion in Rick's eyes as he sat there staring at her. She was wearing a layer of sweet floral dusting powder and her Yukata kimono. The indigo fish on the traditional batik-printed cotton material actually wiggled slightly, mirroring Holly's trembling. The robe was her favorite, meant to make her feel better. It had been Japanese informal wear for centuries—about as long as she'd wanted Rick. At least, that's how she felt.

And it wasn't *just* wanting. This was something special. So as he sat there, the needy hunger apparent in his dark blue eyes, she simply held open her arms.

He was there a heartbeat later, holding her so tightly she could barely breathe. She wrapped her arms around him with equal fervor as he buried his face in the wild disarray of her hair.

The bathroom doorway where they stood was conveniently located right next to her bedroom doorway. Gently sweeping her up in his arms, Rick carried her those last few steps over a new threshold in their relationship.

Bracing one knee on the sweetheart quilt covering her double bed, he set her on the bed with exquisite care. He placed his hands on either side of her head and huskily murmured, "I haven't had two clear thoughts since I first tasted your mouth."

Lowering his head, he tasted her mouth again. His kiss was slow, sweet and enticing. He was persuasive, although there was no need to be. He was tender when she expected him to be impatient. Holly's heart melted.

She returned his kiss with passionate certainty. The tempo changed as he responded by deepening the pressure of his mouth on hers. Fumbling with the sash on her robe, Rick murmured his frustration. Holly echoed the emotion, and her hands immediately joined forces with his to undo the troublesome encumbrance.

Leaning away from her, he slowly opened her robe, as if he were savoring the unwrapping of a precious gift. She shivered from the force of her emotions.

"Are you cold?" he asked.

"Does it feel like I'm cold?" she huskily countered, placing his hand on her breast.

"No." His voice was as husky as hers. "You feel like hot silk."

A moment later his mouth was where his hand had been, claiming the rosy peak. The touch of his tongue on her sensitive skin was amazingly exciting. She felt the impact clear down to her toes, which curled. Spearing her fingers through his dark hair, she held him close—expressing her pleasures with soft murmurs and breathless sighs. He was devilishly creative and he soon had her arching her back clear off the bed with the force of her delight. Her movement created a friction against their lower torsos. Like the strike of a match, her actions started a fire that couldn't be put out.

Patience was a thing of the past. Teasing tenderness became passionate eagerness. The time was now. Holly wrestled with the sleeves of her robe as Rick wrestled with the buttons on his shirt, all the while kissing him as if having her mouth on his was a life-sustaining necessity.

Moments later, she welcomed the feel of his bare chest against her bare breasts with a throaty purr of pleasure. Finally. It was as if she'd waited forever for this moment, as if she'd known the joy would be this remarkably intense. Holly could feel the thud of his heart pounding against her.

Their kisses blended together into a compendium of expressive desire. One after the other, without interruption.

Unwilling to lift his lips from hers, Rick felt his way over the curves of her body, marveling at the softness of her skin, the seeming fragility of her bones.

"My God! You could have been killed," he growled. "You could have been run over. It was a damn fool thing to do!" he raged at her in between kisses as soft as thistledown.

"It's okay," she kept saying, running her hands down his spine in soothing yet sexy slides. "It's okay."

"It's not okay," he muttered, kissing the valley between her breasts. He could feel the vibration of her throaty laughter.

"You're right," she agreed. "It's not okay. It's *incredible*."

Turning his head slightly, he lapped at the creamy curve of her breast with his tongue. "Incredible," he murmured in agreement.

Words were soon abandoned for action as the few remaining articles of clothing separating them were quickly discarded. The telltale humming she felt whenever he touched her increased to a fever pitch. She had to have him with her, within her.

He clearly felt the same way as his movements took on a new urgency. Rolling away from her, he took care of their protection. The moment the condom was on, he came to her in a heated rush.

As he joined with her, Rick looked into Holly's eyes, watching her reaction. It was incredibly erotic, but no more so than the powerful surge of his body.

Holly felt her inner muscles tensing and then rippling with delicate tremors. So fast, it was coming so fast! Gasping his name, she wrapped her legs around him.

Each thrust propelled her to another level of delight. Slide, rush. Slide, rush. She was out of control—clenching, pulsing, throbbing.

And then it came, the peak . . . drowning her in waves of ecstasy. For infinite moments frozen in time, splashes of pleasure continued to lap at her inner shores with successive swells.

He was still poised above her when she felt him stiffen. Her fingers registered the tremors as he froze: head tilted back, eyes closed, his features etched with raw ecstasy. Watching him, Holly smiled at the unexpected wealth of her feminine power. And then her eyes widened as her tremors grew again, her exclamation of surprised delight coinciding with his shout of satisfaction.

When it was all over, Holly instinctively knew that something new was just beginning . . . and that nothing in her life would ever be the same again.

Nine

"There's something I need to tell you...." Rick murmured, trailing a caressing finger down her arm. It was after nine and they'd already missed dinner in the dining hall. Instead they'd raided Holly's refrigerator before returning to bed.

"Something you need to tell me? What is it?"

For one brief moment in time, Rick was tempted to tell her the truth...that he'd been sent by her father to bring her back to Seattle. But that impulse quickly faded given the reality of what her reaction would be. So instead he said, "Uh, it's about your tools."

"I've never heard them referred to like that before," Holly noted with one of her irreverent grins.

Realizing that his hand had traveled to the curve of her breast, Rick had to smile himself. "These are incredible, but I really was talking about your tools. The ones you keep in that carpetbag."

"Are you going to suggest some wickedly creative new use for a wrench?" she inquired.

"No. I was going to suggest that you store your tools elsewhere."

"Really." Her inflection held no hint of a question.

"Yes, really. A carpetbag is no place for tools. Those things hold moisture and promote rust. It's not an appropriate storage place."

"Not appropriate, hmm?"

"No way."

"What about this. . . ." She reached out to intimately caress him. "Is this appropriate?"

"Are we still talking about storing tools?" he inquired with a growl.

"Let's say we're talking about appropriate and inappropriate handling—" she slid her hand first up and then down his tautly throbbing arousal "—of your. . . umm, tools."

"This particular tool needs special handling." Rick reached down to show her what he meant.

"And I'll bet it needs a special covering . . . to protect it from rust, of course," she murmured with a sexy smile. "Let's see how well I can do that. . . ."

She did that so well that by the time she was done, Rick was just about ready to blow a gasket.

"Time for this tool to go to work," Rick grated.

With one powerful thrust, he surged into her with a sensual intensity that rocked her to the core. She raised her hips to take him even farther into her depths. His creative moves soon had Holly gasping with pleasure, and words deserted her as blind ecstasy washed over her.

Much later, when it was finally all over, she lay in his arms, limp as a dishrag. Her smile was that of a cat who'd not only eaten the cream, but had a patent on it. "You're definitely a master craftsman, Rick," she whispered. "No doubt about that."

Maybe not, but Rick had plenty of other doubts regarding just about every other aspect of his life.

"You know how you're always saying that I should take a vacation?" Holly said to Skye early the next morning. The two of them were alone in Skye's kitchen, where she was baking a fresh batch of bread.

"I am?"

"Sure you are." Holly nibbled on a slice of honey wheat bread, still warm from the oven. "Well, I'm going to take your advice and get away. Just for one day. I'll be back by tomorrow evening. I'd appreciate it if you and Guido would take over my classes tomorrow. Think you can do that?"

"Sure we can do that. Where are you going?"

"I'm going camping."

"Sounds great."

"I knew you'd think so. I won't be gone too long. By the way, Rick is coming with me," she mumbled around a mouthful of bread she'd just popped into her mouth.

"What was that again?" Skye inquired.

"Rick is coming with me. He's arranged to take a few days off."

"And you're taking him camping?"

"That's right," Holly said dreamily. "It's gonna be wonderful!" She sighed.

"Somehow I get the impression it already was wonderful," Skye noted wryly. "Why, Holly, you're not actually blushing, are you? You never blush."

"I've never felt this way before," Holly confessed.

"You've got it bad, huh?"

Holly nodded.

"And from the look on Rick's face yesterday when you were almost hit by that truck, I'd say he feels the same way."

"I have reason to believe so, yes," Holly noted demurely.

"I thought so. That's why I ran interference for you last night and assured everybody else you were being well taken care of."

"That's for sure!" The emphatic exclamation was out of Holly's mouth before she'd even thought about it. She looked at Skye hesitantly... and a second later the two of them were laughing aloud.

"So, Holly, care to go into any more detail than that?" Skye teased her.

"Nope."

"What made you decide to go camping with Rick? Aside from the obvious, I mean, so get that grin off your face," Skye chastised her with mock ferocity. "I'm trying to ask you a simple question here. Has he ever been camping before?"

"No. This will be a first for him."

"One of many with you, I hope."

"Thanks, Skye. I knew I could count on your support. And discretion."

"Meaning?"

"I don't want everybody else knowing where I'm going. You know how Byron and Guido are. They'll just make a fuss, give Rick the third degree."

"I thought they'd done that already."

"That was nothing compared to what they'd do if they knew I was intimately involved with Rick. It's too new. I want to have a day or two to savor this to myself first, okay?"

"Okay. But you two will have more than a day or two to enjoy your relationship. I know you, Holly. You wouldn't be getting this involved if you didn't believe that you and Rick had some kind of a future together."

"Hopefully so," Holly said.

"If not, Rick better watch out," Skye warned.

* * *

"Tell me again why we're going camping?" Rick asked as soon as they'd left Inner View.

"Because if we stay at Inner View and Guido catches you sleeping in my cabin, there's a chance he might overreact," Holly said.

"To put it mildly," Rick noted mockingly. "Listen, about this camping thing, you do realize that my idea of roughing it is being more than ten minutes away from a convenience store."

"Time to broaden your horizons, Rick."

"And we couldn't drive in my car...?"

"Because the road where we're going is too rough. Consider yourself lucky I'm letting you drive my jeep. I'm very fond of this baby. I don't let just anyone drive her, you know."

"I'm honored, I'm sure, to be driving a bright yellow vehicle that resembles a bumblebee."

"Listen, your car isn't exactly racing-car material. It's the most nondescript car I've ever seen."

Which is exactly why Rick drove it.

"Besides, I'm also graciously allowing you to listen to a baseball game on the radio," Holly pointed out. "Sounds like Greek to me, however."

"That's because of the static. Bad reception up here in the mountains."

"It's not the reception. It's the game. Maybe you should explain it to me."

"You know how you always have all these quotes you're telling me? Well I've got one for you on baseball. I even know the guy's name. Paul Dickson. And he said this about baseball. 'It's like church. Many attend, but few understand.'"

"Meaning you don't know what the rules are, either."

"Of course I know the rules. But they're too complicated..."

"For li'l ol' me to understand?" She batted her eyelashes at him.

"It's a guy thing."

"Like your interest in the well-being of my tools?"

"Exactly."

"Well, if it makes you feel better, you can keep the secrets of your little game to yourself. I prefer football, anyway."

Rick was astonished with this piece of news. "You like football?"

"Sure. Why else do you think I was quoting a football coach to you earlier? Now there's a game!"

"But it's violent."

"Well, that can be a drawback, I admit."

"Aren't you a pacifist or something? You jumped on my case for that fight I was in."

"Your *case* wasn't the only thing I jumped all over, if you'll recall," she noted with a saucy grin. "The truth is that I don't condone violence. But I like football. Go figure. If you'll recall, I never claimed to be logical."

"Even on your worst days, no one could accuse you of being logical," Rick agreed.

"Of course, I actually am logical in my own way—to my own logic—but I meant logical in the narrow, preconceived concept of the word."

"Whatever you say."

"I say we turn right up ahead. Slow down.... Here, we turn right here."

"This isn't a road. It's a dirt path."

"That's why we're driving a four-wheel-drive vehicle and not your car. Just go slowly and we'll do fine."

Rick planned on going slowly with her, making love to her until morning once they got to their campsite.

"We're here," Holly announced a short time later.

"This is where we're camping?" Rick asked, looking around at the dense forest.

"No. This is where we start backpacking."

"We start what?"

"Walking and carrying the packs I've got in the back."

"Walk? How far?"

"Only half a mile. You're gonna love it! Out in nature, enjoying the great outdoors, cuddling up together near an open fire. Sharing our sleeping bags. It's going to be great!"

"So you keep telling me."

"If the pack is too heavy for you . . ." she began.

"Give it here." He grabbed it from her.

"You're going to love the view from our campsite," she said as she slid her own backpack on.

"I prefer looking at you."

"I *was* referring to me." She gave him one of her sassy grins.

"Got something up your sleeve, do you?" he inquired.

"Yes. Insect repellent. Here, put some on your arms, too."

"That wasn't exactly what I had in mind, Holly." To himself, Rick wondered who in their right mind would want to do this kind of stuff on a regular basis—smear themselves with insect repellent, carry a two-ton pack on their back and walk around a bunch of trees. He needed some inspiration here. "Tell me more about the view."

"There are no obstructions, no distractions. Just lots of bare . . . landscape . . . to be explored."

"Bare, huh?"

"Except for a bit of black satin. . . ."

"In that case, what are we waiting for?" He took her hand and tugged her along after him. "Come on. Let's go check this *view* out!"

"We don't have to rush. The view isn't going anyplace," she reminded him.

"I know. That's the problem. Can't you and your *view* walk a little faster?"

"Half the fun of backpacking is enjoying the trail, Rick. Communing with nature."

"Are you sure we're going to have this campsite all to ourselves?" Rick asked.

"Yes. It's private property. No trespassing allowed."

"Then why are *we* here?"

"Because I own the property. Actually, the Institute for Creative Development owns the property. And since you're with the director, I wouldn't worry about it. The only thing we do have to worry about is staying away from poison oak, although I've never actually seen any up here."

"A motel is looking better all the time."

"You can't get this kind of peace and quiet in a motel. You don't get Douglas fir and Western red cedar soaring free, trying to touch the sky. You don't get dappled light filtering over the forest floor. In motels, you get orange shag carpeting and dusty ceilings. Here you've got glacier-fed streams and clean air. And nothing but the stars over your head at night."

"I thought we were sleeping in a tent."

"I did bring along a tent. You're carrying it."

Along with a cabin full of other stuff, Rick thought to himself. Or that's how it felt.

"You sure that pack isn't too heavy?" Holly asked.

"It's fine. I carry stuff twice this heavy all the time."

"We're almost there," she assured him.

"No problem."

In fact, by the time they arrived at the campsite, Rick was feeling very Neanderthal. Maybe Holly was right. There might be something to this camping stuff, after all. He felt like a great explorer, the last of the mountain men. Just him against nature. Daniel Boone with a backpack.

"You go start dinner and I'll put up the tent," Rick declared, sliding the backpack off like a pro.

"Are you sure? Have you ever put up a tent before?"

"Come on, Holly. We're not talking brain surgery here. How hard can it be?"

Rick soon discovered it was harder than hooking up his multichannel stereo system or even setting the timing on his car engine. He wasn't about to admit defeat, however. No piece of canvas and pile of poles was gonna get the better of him. Not in this lifetime.

"You sure you don't want help, Rick?" Holly called out from her place over by the campfire. She'd managed to gather wood, get the fire going and start dinner while he was still on stage one of the tent-pitching procedure. "I could help...."

"No way," he growled even as another tent stake came undone from the ground.

Eventually he succeeded in getting the thing put up. Dusting off his hands, he proudly showed off his construction project to Holly. "See, I told you I could do it. No problem."

"It looks great," Holly said, even though the tent was slightly lopsided. "Are you ready for dinner?"

"Sure am. What are we eating?"

"Fire food."

"Which is?"

"Veggie kebabs, fire-baked potatoes, tofu hot dogs, and for dessert...roasted marshmallows."

They sat on a timeworn log in front of the fire, knees bent, shoulders touching as they ate their camp dinner. They lingered over dessert, the popping sounds of the fire a soothing accompaniment to their nibbling. It didn't take long, however, before their attention turned from nibbling on food to nibbling one another.

It started with Rick sampling the supple curve of her throat. For once, she wore a small earring that didn't get in his way, although the silver dolphin did appear to be poised in her earlobe. Still it was relatively easy to nibble his way around her earring to the sensitive skin surrounding her ear.

Holly shivered. Her senses were humming again, and he wasn't even really kissing her yet! Making love with him hadn't lessened her attraction to him. It had only strengthened it.

But that was because she wasn't just attracted to him. This was much more than that. This was about wanting to take care of him when he was sick, wanting to make sure he was never lonely again, wanting to see his face on the pillow beside her every morning.

Leaning away from her, he gazed into her eyes. She wondered if he could read her thoughts and made no effort to hide them from him. The flickering firelight added an even more devilish cast to Rick's naughty grin as he slowly undid the buttons on her scooped-neck lilac top.

"That fire is making me warm," he noted. "How about you?"

"*This* fire is making me warm," she countered, sliding her hand over the placket of his jeans. "Don't you feel hot?"

He growled his affirmative reply.

"Then you should take your shirt off." She helped him with that, their fingers bumping into one another as they both wrestled with the buttons.

Holly had already set out the sleeping bags near the fire. It was a simple matter to move from the log to softer territory. Rick, too, was moving on to softer territory, exploring the creamy softness of her breast with his teasing tongue.

With his help, she wiggled out of her purple jeans and then returned the favor by helping him shimmy out of his jeans.

Lying beside him, Holly drew a road map over invisible highways on his chest. East to west. Side to side. From his collarbone south to his navel. "Your belly button is an innie."

"I want to be innie you," Rick grated.

"What's stopping you?"

"This...." He tossed her black satin underwear over his shoulder.

"And this...." She tossed his underwear over her shoulder before helping to sheath him in a condom.

And then he came to her. "Innie..." He surged upward. "Outie..." He withdrew. "Innie..." He came to her again.

"You're wicked," Holly purred with delighted pleasure.

"Yeah."

"I like a little of that in a man," she murmured breathlessly.

"Only a little?"

"More...oh, Rick...yes! Yes! Just like that."

"You're being bossy again," he growled.

She smiled up at him, tightening around him with sultry seductiveness. "Are you complaining?"

"No way!"

The pleasure was getting so intense that Holly couldn't concentrate enough to speak. She could only gasp. She was spiraling upward, like a leaf caught in a whirlwind, as their bodies glided together in a silent yet deeply lyrical cadence. There was a moment in time when she was poised on the very brink of ecstasy. That's when Rick reached down and touched her in such a way that she immediately climaxed and the stars from the heavens above showered down around her.

* * *

"I can't believe we did that out here in the open," Holly murmured light years later.

"I thought you said this was private property."

"It is. But I've never done anything like this before."

"Me, either," Rick admitted. "I gotta tell you, this makes me wonder why I didn't try camping before."

"It's not just camping," she reprimanded him with a gentle sock to his arm. "It's the person you're with."

"It certainly is. The very special, incredibly sexy and creative person I'm with."

"Which reminds me, I never told you about the four stages of creativity, did I? Don't give me that face. I think you're going to enjoy this lesson. Actually it's better if I show you, rather than tell you. The first stage is effort." Holly kissed Rick's still-bruised knuckles, the inside of his wrist, his elbow, his shoulder.

"You mean effort like this...?" He shifted her hair back from her face before letting his fingers trail down her cheek, under her chin and then down her neck to the valley between her breasts.

"Just like that," she confirmed huskily, gasping as he nipped her bare shoulder with his teeth.

He touched her as if he were a blind man and she held the secrets of life written in braille. The hollow behind her knee, the curvy instep of her bare foot—every one of her body's many curves and inlets was explored and treasured.

Need quickly flared, and after donning protection, he was soon within her again as she sat perched above him. "Stage two is—" she lifted up "—withdrawal."

Groaning, he tugged her down.

"Stage three ... insight. Mental penetration." She leaned down, smoothing his hair back from his forehead and kissing him with burning honesty, her tongue dueling with his, mimicking the erotic thrusts taking place elsewhere.

"And finally... elaboration," she whispered.

"I'll take care of that one," Rick growled, shifting so they were both on their sides. Taking her bent knee in his hand, he lifted her leg up over his hip. Their new position allowed for even more pleasure, as each thrust took him even deeper. "Elaborate enough for you?"

"Mmm. I knew you were the creative type. You catch on fast."

"Fast?" He turned again so that she was beneath him and increased the tempo. "Like that?"

"I love it!" she gasped. "I'm gonna... I'm gonna..."

"I know you are." His grin was wicked.

"...scream!"

He let her. There was no one around but him to hear her feminine cry of satisfaction or his own shout of completion a short time later.

Afterward, when Holly had regained enough breath to finally form a complete sentence again, she smoothed a dark lock of hair out of his eyes and whispered, "I love you."

Startled, Rick stared down into her eyes. Her face was flushed with sensual satisfaction, her gaze dreamy and tender. "You don't have to look so shocked about it," she gently reprimanded him. "It's okay. You don't have to say anything. It's just that I'm not very good at keeping my emotions to myself."

Without further ado, Holly snuggled against him and minutes later was sound asleep in the cozy cocoon of their joined sleeping bags.

It wasn't that simple for Rick, who lay there long into the night, holding her protectively in his arms, wondering why he ever thought this case would be simple. He'd never run into anything more complicated in his life.

Holly was already up and about when Rick finally woke up the next morning. The smell of fresh coffee was a welcome scent. He'd been afraid she was going to make him drink one of her herbal teas. A mug of black coffee, a splash in the creek, and Rick was wide awake. His jeans looked the worse for wear after spending the night in the dirt so he'd opted to put on a clean pair of khaki slacks he'd brought along as backup. After rolling up the sleeves of his white shirt, he was ready to face the world—and the woman who claimed she loved him.

She was sitting on a blanket, curled up like a pretzel.

"What are you doing?" he asked, sitting next to her and stretching his legs straight out.

"I'm doing my morning yoga." She inhaled one final, calming breath. "I'm done now."

"Good. You're too far away." He tugged her onto his lap so that she straddled his legs and faced him. The navy blue tights she was wearing fit her like a second skin, while her red top lovingly followed her curves.

Curving her hands around his neck, she leaned forward to kiss him. It was an eloquent expression of the wealth of her love for him, and she tasted the answering passion in his response. Exultant, she sat back and grinned first at him and then up at the blue sky lightly streaked with high cirrus clouds. "Isn't it a beautiful day? The most beautiful day in the world. We've even got a Sisley sky," she declared. "Definitely Sisley."

"Did you say Sisley? Or drizzly?"

"Sisley. A French impressionist painter who was known for his beautiful skies."

"You know a lot about art, don't you?"

Holly nodded. "It was one of my favorite subjects in school, much to my father's dismay. He didn't approve. Considered art a waste of time. My father doesn't like wasting time. Or money. I was always a big disappointment to him. In fact, I remember him once saying to me, 'Why couldn't you have been a better daughter and more help to me. Someone I could be proud of.' "

Rick swore softly but vehemently under his breath.

"It was a long time ago," Holly said. "My mother had been dead for almost a year, so I must have been about nine at the time. Those were the days when I used to long for a large family. I even wrote second cousins to try and establish a bond. It didn't work. So I eventually went out and got my own family—a family of my choosing." Realizing how that sounded, Holly corrected herself. "Actually, I didn't just go out and *get* them. That sounds as if family is a commodity you can go out and get like a gallon of milk or a loaf of bread, and that's not the case at all. I've been fortunate enough to end up with an extended family of my own, and I'm very grateful for that."

Noticing the brooding look on Rick's face, Holly assumed he didn't feel comfortable with all this talk about family, not having one himself, so she quickly changed the subject by asking him how he wanted his eggs done for breakfast.

As she bustled around the relit campfire, Rick remembered one of the first things Holly had said to him. "There's nothing I hate more than being lied to," she'd told him that first day he'd come to Inner View. How long ago it seemed to him now. So much had changed. But some things remained the same. Like the fact that she didn't know the truth about him. Didn't know who he really was.

Rick had to tell her, he knew that. And soon. At least he'd broken off the deal with her father in that fateful phone call right before Holly had rushed in front of a truck and almost gotten herself killed. Rick hoped the fact that he'd done that would make Holly realize he wasn't all bad, despite his having lied to her.

But he couldn't bring himself to spoil this special time they had together. He wanted—no he *needed*—to strengthen the bond between them before he told her the truth. A few more hours. That's all he was asking for here. Just a few more hours.

All too soon it was time to go back to Inner View, and Rick still hadn't told Holly the truth. After breakfast he'd opted for kissing her instead of talking to her, and they'd ended up making love again. He knew it was selfish of him, but he couldn't risk threatening what they had together—not at that vulnerable moment.

All during the drive Rick tried to come up with a suitable way of breaking the news to her. Before he knew it, they were pulling up in front of the Inner View office, and he still hadn't found the right words.

Charity rushed out to greet them the moment they drove up. "I'm so glad you're back!"

"What happened?" Holly asked worriedly. "Is the baby all right?"

"She's fine," Charity said.

Holly relaxed. "Then what is it? Did the copier get jammed again?" she teasingly asked, knowing she was the only one who had the magic touch with the machine.

"No, that's not it."

"Did the computers go down?"

"No," Charity replied. "But someone claiming to be Mr. Richard Potter is on the phone, demanding to know what's going on here!"

Ten

The jig was up. Rick knew that the moment he heard Charity's comment.

"Obviously there's some kind of mistake," Holly began.

"Holly, I need to talk to you," Rick said urgently.

"Sure. Just let me clear up this misunderstanding first."

Grabbing her arm, he pulled her aside. "It's not a misunderstanding. Well, it is, but . . . Hell, Holly. I'm not Rick Potter."

"What?"

"Potter isn't my real name. It's Rick Dunbar."

The name meant nothing to her. "What is this? Why would you pretend to be Mr. Potter?"

"I think we should talk without an audience, don't you?" Rick said, indicating Charity, who'd now been joined by Skye.

"Tell the man on the phone that I'll call him back," Holly told Charity. To Rick she said, "We'll talk in my cabin."

Holly didn't even wait to close her front door before saying, "What's this all about?"

"Your father," Rick said bluntly. "He hired me to find you and bring you back to him."

Holly sat down on the couch before she fell down. "What are you saying?" Her voice was shaky and strained.

"I'm a private investigator. My name is Rick Dunbar. I tracked you up here."

"I don't believe this!" Holly shook her head, as if doubting she'd heard him correctly. "My father hired you to track me down like some kind of animal?"

"I wouldn't put it that way—"

"I'm sure you wouldn't. I'm sure you were just following orders. My father's real good at giving those." Holly could feel something inside of her curling up and dying. Shame washed over her. "Did my father tell you to sleep with me, too? Was that part of the grand scheme? Did you think you could seduce me into returning to my father? That you'd be able to wrap me around your finger and I'd obediently trail after you back to Daddy, like a good little girl, is that it?"

"No, that's not it!" Rick growled. "Making love with you had nothing to do with your father."

"Do you really expect me to believe that?"

"It's the truth. Look, I was going to tell you about this earlier—"

"Sure you were. That's one of the problems with lying, Rick. No one believes anything you say anymore. If there's one thing I've learned over the years, it's that people are never sneaky in just one area of their life. Dishonesty and deceit tend to recur over and over. Well, it's not going to recur with me. It's over. You can drop the act now."

"Dammit, Holly. It wasn't an act!"

"It was on my part. I wanted to teach you a lesson. Aha, now you're the one surprised, right?"

"What are you talking about?"

"You're not the only one with a hidden agenda. I thought it was time a woman taught you a thing or two, brought you down a peg or two."

Rick glared at her. "You told me that you loved me. Are you saying you were lying?"

"You thought you held the monopoly on deception?" she countered.

"You don't lie, Holly. You told me so yourself."

"The man I said those words to doesn't exist except in my foolish imagination. Because I could never love a man who's done what you've done, Rick. I could never love a slick con artist who'll do anything for a buck."

"No? Well, you gave a pretty damn good impression of it just a few hours ago, honey." His words vibrated with unadulterated male rage.

"I didn't know the truth then," she retorted with equal anger. "I do now. All I can say is that I hope my father is paying you plenty for this job, Rick. You've certainly earned every penny!"

The look he gave her would have scorched a hole straight through her heart, had it not already been broken into tiny pieces.

"That's right, lady. Some of us actually have to work for a living. We have to earn money because we weren't born with silver spoons in our mouths. You can fall back on that poor little rich girl routine all you want, but your problems are puny compared to the trouble that's out there. There are people living out on the street in cardboard boxes. Now *they*'ve got problems. All you've got is a stubborn determination not to look past the end of your nose."

"Maybe if I'd looked past the end of my nose I'd have seen you for what you are," she shot back.

"And maybe you *did* see me for what I am," Rick retorted before turning on his heel and walking out, slamming the door after him.

The sound made her jump. Like the shattering of glass, her anger disintegrated into shards of pain. The numbness she'd experienced when he'd first told her he'd been sent by her father had worn off. Now there was nothing left but pain and despair.

Rick tossed his suitcase into the back of his car without even bothering to zip it all the way closed. He was out of here! This place had been nothing but trouble since he'd first stepped foot here.

He'd been on the verge of telling Holly about that phone call he'd made to her father, taking himself off the case, when she'd floored him with the news that she'd been playing him for a fool. Thank God he hadn't admitted how much of a fool—ten thousand dollars' worth. The fee he'd given up for her. Not to mention what else he'd been tempted to give up for her. Precious things, like his independence, maybe even his heart.

Rick slammed the back door shut. Turning around, he almost tripped over Asia. Great. Just what he needed. She smiled at him. He didn't smile back. He wasn't fooled. Women started early with their feminine wiles, sneaking their way into your heart so they could stomp on it. This kid was no exception. Fifteen years down the road, she'd be creating havoc with some poor unsuspecting slob.

"I gotta go potty," Asia announced.

Rick didn't blink an eye. "We've all got problems, kid."

She yanked on his slacks. He was about to tell her to keep her grimy little mitts to herself when she wrapped her arms around his leg and gave him a hug. Turning her angelic face up to his, she simply said, "I like you." Then she let go and skipped away, taking a tiny piece of Rick's heart with her.

"You'll get over it, kid," he muttered. "And so will I."

* * *

Holly wasn't sure how long she sat there on the couch, wiping away the tears that refused to stop, when the phone rang.

"Holly, it's Charity. Are you okay? I just saw Rick driving past the office as if the devil himself was after him."

"I'm okay," Holly huskily replied. "My instincts stink, but I'm okay."

"You don't sound okay. It sounds like you've been crying."

"I was, but I'm stopping now." Sniffing, Holly grabbed a facial tissue and wiped away her tears. "I'm definitely stopping now."

"What's the matter?"

"You know that call from Mr. Potter? Well, it seems we've been had." Holly ironically noted that she'd been *had* in the most intimate way possible...and Rick had been paid to do it. "The man who was calling himself Rick Potter was an impostor. My father sent him to track me down."

"Oh, Holly, no!"

"Oh, Holly, yes," she countered bitterly. "Pretty incredible, huh? I can't believe I didn't see what was going on. There were clues, Charity. He didn't look the part of an analytical number cruncher. He didn't even attempt to play that role. Instead he boldly reprimanded us for stereotyping him. He's got chutzpah, I'll give him that much." The problem was that Holly had given Rick much more than that—her faith, her love, her heart.

"What are you going to do?" Charity asked her.

"I'm going to call Mr. Potter back, apologize and offer his company a voucher for two free seminars. And I'm going to institute a new policy of checking ID on every incoming participant. And then I'm going to get on with my life."

Holly knew it wouldn't be long before word of what happened got around Inner View. Within five minutes after her hanging up the phone with Charity, Skye came knocking on Holly's door.

"I just heard what happened," Skye said. "I brought some of my special lemon mint tea for you."

"So much for my great instincts, huh?" Holly couldn't help it, the tears started again, rolling down her face and landing with a wet plop on the pad of paper on which she was making a list. *Getting on with my life: Things to do* was the now-damp title.

Skye sat next to her on the couch and hugged her consolingly.

"What about the kids?" Holly sniffed. "Aren't you supposed to be in class?"

"Guido's taking care of the class. Good thing, too," Skye muttered. "Otherwise Rick would never have gotten out of here alive."

"You're a pacifist, Skye," Holly reminded her. "You don't even approve of football."

"Football is just a game. This is personal."

"Yeah, very personal. It's still not sinking in completely. But I'm okay. I'm going to be just fine." The lead in the pencil Holly was doodling with cracked under the pressure she'd applied to it. Holly focused all her attention on the broken tip. How suddenly it had cracked off, just as suddenly as her heart had cracked. She studied it closely because doing so kept the tears at bay and she was tired of crying. "Ever wonder how they get the lead in pencils?"

"Now I know you're not okay yet," Skye noted worriedly. "You only do your trivia thing when you're really upset."

Holly recalled the other two times recently when she'd gone into her "trivia thing," as Skye put it. The first had been when Rick had accompanied her into the kitchen when she'd made tea and she'd ended up giving him a rundown on the complete history of tea making. The second had been when they'd gone to Paradise and she'd rattled off a lot of facts about Mount Rainier. Of course, he'd been sitting right next to her at the time, his thigh warm against hers.

"Go ahead," Skye said. "I know it makes you feel better. How do they put the lead in pencils?"

"I don't have a clue." Holly sighed glumly. "That seems to sum up how I feel right now. Like I don't have a clue. Like I'm an idiot for being taken in by Rick's deception."

"We were all taken in."

"Not Guido. He never really fell for Rick's act. And you were suspicious, too. I should have listened to the two of you."

"You listened to your heart, Holly, and no one can fault you for that."

"I can."

"You're always being too hard on yourself."

"If I'd been harder on myself, I would have been more cautious."

"I wish there was something I could say to make you feel better," Skye said.

Trying to make her feel better seemed the order of the evening. For dinner, Whit made Holly's favorite meal: ratatouille. Knowing he'd put a lot of work into it, she tried to do more than pick at her food, but it was difficult.

Guido's way of making her feel better was to give her one of his special giant bear hugs. "Damn number cruncher." Guido's gravelly voice was a comforting growl in her ear. "I smelled something fishy about him all along. I'm sorry, Holly. I should have followed up on my suspicions. Checked him out or something."

"It's not your fault, Guido."

"It's not yours, either. It's that damn father of yours.... Pardon my French."

"You've been more of a father to me than he ever was," Holly noted with a grateful kiss to Guido's cheek. "And I appreciate it, Guido."

"Go on now," he muttered. "You're gonna make me blush."

"And you're gonna make me cry, so I guess it's time we called it quits for tonight, huh?" Holly said with a wobbly grin.

"Guess so." He gave her another hug before letting her go. "You sleep tight now, you hear?"

But all Holly heard that night was the sound of painful memories running like a never-ending movie loop in her head. The haunting voices of self-derision and regret sent her outside to the hopeful comfort of her dilapidated rocking chair.

It was raining, a fitting accompaniment to the tears still falling inside her soul. She hadn't been able to stay in her bedroom. She couldn't look at the soft pastel colors of the sweetheart quilt on her bed without remembering the way Rick had set her on that quilt before making love to her.

That seemed to be all she was doing tonight. Remembering. Remembering every kiss, every incident. Remembering the scene at the potter's wheel when Rick had said, "It'll do whatever you want, if you don't push it too far."

Looking back, knowing what she knew now, Holly wondered if Rick had really been talking about the clay at all. Or had he been referring to her? Sweet-talk her, charm her, treat *her* gently and *she* would do whatever he wanted—if he didn't push her too far?

Well, by God, he had pushed her too far. Much too far. Making love to her was reprehensible. A low-down, cheap and dirty trick—even for a scoundrel con man like Rick.

But Holly was the one who felt cheap and dirty, for falling for his hustling routine. For falling for him. For falling into his trap and inviting him into her bed.

In the end, all she'd been inviting was disaster. Of all the things her father had said or done to her, and there had been quite a catalog throughout the years, this was by far the worst.

As for Rick...words couldn't come close to describing the feeling of betrayal she was experiencing right now. She remembered him warning her that he was no knight in shining armor. How right he'd been. And how foolish of her not to have believed him.

"Hey, boss, I didn't expect you back tonight!" Vin exclaimed when Rick walked into his office.

"Get your feet off my desk!" Rick growled. "And get the hell out of my chair."

"Oh-oh. Things didn't go so good for you up there in the mountains, huh?" Vin noted as he quickly vacated Rick's turf.

"That's an understatement if ever I heard one," Rick retorted as he sat in his desk chair. It was the one good piece of office furniture he owned. Leather. The real thing. None of that Naugahyde stuff. "What are you doing lounging around here, anyway? I don't pay you to read comic books and sleep at my desk. Do it again and you're fired."

"It's a good thing I know you don't mean it, or I'd be upset," Vin said.

"I do mean it," Rick stubbornly maintained.

"You're such a kidder, boss."

"What's that sleeping bag doing here?" Rick demanded, having just caught sight of it. He glared at it as if it were a malevolent snake, reminding him as it did of his time with Holly at their campsite.

"Well, you see, it's like this, boss. My mother, she got mad at me for mouthing back to her. So she kind of kicked me out."

"Tell me another one. I've met your mother. You're her pride and joy. She'd never throw you out."

"Okay, she didn't exactly throw me out. We had a big fight over this girl I'm seeing."

"How long have you been sleeping here?"

"Only two days. You gonna kick me out, boss?" Vin asked worriedly.

"Your mother know where you are?"

"Are you kidding? My mother knows everything. She's got a spy network like you wouldn't believe."

Leaning back in his chair, Rick made a weary gesture with his hand. "You can stay."

"Gee, thanks, boss. You're the greatest."

"Yeah, right." The greatest what? Rick wondered. The greatest liar? The greatest lover? Or the greatest fool who'd ever walked the face of the earth? Had Holly been telling the truth when she said she didn't love him, that she'd only wanted to bring him down a peg or two?

"You got trouble?" Vin asked him in commiseration.

"Yeah, I got trouble, all right. The worst kind. Heart trouble." Now, what had made him put it that way? Rick irritably wondered. He should have said woman trouble. But it felt worse than that....

"I heard they got medicine for heart trouble, boss," Vin earnestly informed him.

"Not for what ails me, Vin."

"It's that serious? Is it gonna kill you?"

"Naw. I'm a tough SOB. Don't you know that? Nothing's gonna kill me. I'm invincible." Having said the words, Rick only wished he could believe them.

The next morning, after a frustrating yoga meditation session, Holly deliberately dressed in her most cheerful colors. Her brightly colored shirt displayed just about every hue of the rainbow in its Hawaiian print. Her pants were poppy red, with a paper-bag-style elastic waist that made them very comfortable to wear when she was working with the children—bending and moving around a lot.

As she slipped on a pair of funky earrings shaped like giant red lips, Holly was determined to channel all her attention onto the children. They needed her. She wouldn't let them down, the way she'd been let down. She planned on being there for them.

But kids had a sixth sense about these things. They noticed right away that something wasn't right with Holly.

"You're too happy. Something's wrong. You look like my mom did when my dad went to prison," Bobby told Holly. "She was too happy then. Not a *real* happy. Just a fake one to make me feel better."

"I'm just sad today, Bobby," Holly admitted. "Everybody gets sad sometimes. It makes the days we feel good look even better. Like having it rain makes us appreciate the sunshine even more."

"Yeah, but does it have to rain sooo much?" Larry countered.

"Look at this, Holly," the normally shy Martha exclaimed. "I really like this picture I painted. It's you eating ice cream at Paradise."

Holly remembered the day all too well. Rick sitting next to her, seducing her with his eyes, courting her with his touch, and all the while deceiving her.

"Don't you like it?" Martha asked Holly.

"It's wonderful, Martha." The girl had indeed come very far from the stick figures she'd been drawing just a week ago. Her drawing was three-dimensional, and she'd taken special care with the shape of the ice-cream cone. "You did a great job!"

Martha rewarded her with a shy smile. "I did, didn't I?"

"You bet."

"I did a great job, too," Jordan announced. "I've decided I'm going to be an artist when I grow up. It's in my blood."

"Mine, too. This picture is too good to give away. I'm going to keep this one for me," Martha decided.

"You do that," Holly said. "Hang on to things that are important to you. Don't give them away without thinking. Take special care of them." Holly only wished she'd taken special care and not given her heart to Rick so foolishly. "If wishes were horses, all men could ride," she muttered.

"What did you say, Holly?"

"Nothing, Martha. Nothing."

"You're not the only one crying today," Byron informed Holly later that afternoon as he joined her for a cup of lemon mint tea.

"What are you talking about?" Holly asked.

"I'm talking about Charity. She's very upset about what happened."

"What on earth for?"

"It seems she feels responsible because she was the one who told you about the real Mr. Potter being on the phone."

"There's no need for her to feel responsible. Getting bad news is no reason to kill the messenger."

"Tell that to Charity."

"I will."

"I didn't want to say anything given your situation, but... well... actually, the two of us have kind of gotten closer the past few days."

"I'm so glad to hear that, Byron. I was wondering how long it would take for you to wake up and smell the coffee," Holly teased him, glad that things were working out romantically for *someone*, since they certainly weren't for her.

Byron grinned and shrugged self-consciously. "A beautiful girl like her...I didn't think she'd be interested in someone in a wheelchair, other than in a strictly platonic way."

"Shame on you," she gently chastised him. "I thought you knew better than that."

"I wasn't sure she'd want a man like me."

"A man like you, Byron?" Holly repeated indignantly. "Listen, plenty of women would want a man like you. Trust me. You're an honest man. A good man. A damn sexy, good-looking man with a wonderful sense of humor and a heart of gold. You're the best, Byron. And I don't want to hear you say otherwise."

"Yes, ma'am."

That was what Rick had said to her. Holly winced inside at the memory. "You and Charity have a lot of things going for you. You're both good, decent people who would never lie to make a buck."

"Unlike Rick Dunbar, hmm?"

"That's right. Guido was right to be suspicious of him."

"I'm not so sure," Byron noted thoughtfully. "I don't think the guy was that good an actor."

"What's that supposed to mean?"

"I think the guy was tied in knots over you. Much as he wanted to deny it. He even did a bust of you in my class. Turned out to be pretty good."

"What happened to it?"

"He smashed it," Byron reluctantly admitted.

"Yeah, well he tried smashing me, too," Holly stated bitterly. "But I'm not going to let him."

"Rick's not the only one at fault here, you know. Your father also played a major role," Byron reminded her.

"I haven't forgotten that. Not for one minute."

"What are you going to do about it?" Byron challenged her.

Holly immediately accepted the challenge. "I'm going to stop stewing up here and go tell my father to keep his private investigators to himself!"

"Good for you, Holly. Go for it!"

She did, driving into Seattle the very next afternoon, as soon as her classes were over. She'd vacillated back and forth about what to wear for an hour. She hadn't seen her father in over five years. She wanted to make a good impression, but she didn't want to dress to please him.

Actually, the truth was Holly didn't know what she wanted or expected from this meeting. She only knew she had to do this. Confront her father with what he'd done. In the end, it didn't really matter what she wore, because she had a feeling he wouldn't like it, regardless of what she chose.

So she selected an outfit that pleased her—a silk-screened skirt designed by a friend of hers. It was a throwback to the fifties in style and content—a full skirt with bright splashes of sliced watermelon against a black background. With it, Holly wore a black shell and a short fuchsia jacket that matched the color of the watermelon slices. Naturally she wore her wooden fruit necklace and her dangly watermelon earrings with it.

The time on her Van Gogh watch was exactly 3:20 p.m. when Holly boldly breezed into her father's office as if her heart wasn't in her throat.

"I understand you're looking for me," she said.

As if on cue, her father said, "Couldn't you have made an effort to dress appropriately for a business meeting?"

"I didn't come here for a business meeting," Holly retorted. "I came here to tell you once and for all to stop trying to run my life!"

"Someone's got to do it."

"For your information, I've been running my own life very successfully for quite some time now. Just because you don't agree with the things I do—"

"Crazy things," her father interrupted her to declare.

"In your opinion."

"You're just like your mother. Always coming up with half-baked ideas."

"Don't you dare insult my mother! If you ask me, she was too good for you."

"I didn't ask you."

"No, you'd never stoop to ask someone else for their opinion. You already have all the wrong answers yourself."

"How dare you talk to your father that way!"

"How dare you send a private investigator after me!" Holly shot back.

"You're just like your mother."

"That's the biggest compliment you've ever given me."

"I didn't mean it as a compliment. If she hadn't been so stupidly naive as to think that she could change the world, she'd still be alive today."

"What are you talking about? My mother was killed in a car accident."

"Driving home from a meeting with one of her stupid charity groups."

"You never told me that before."

"It was none of your business."

"None of my business . . ." Holly sputtered indignantly.

"Your mother left me. I loved her and that was the thanks I got."

"Mother was leaving you?"

"She died, didn't she? That's leaving me."

"She didn't exactly go voluntarily."

"She should have fought harder to stay alive. She shouldn't have been out driving that late to begin with. I strictly forbade her to go out. How dare she disobey me! How dare she leave me, going and dying that way!''

After all these years, Holly could see the anger still emanating from her father. She'd never considered this scenario, that her father would blame her mother for dying. A number of things clicked into place for Holly. She'd always sensed an anger in him regarding her mother, but she'd never been able to figure out its cause. Now she could. Her father had always been a controller, and her mother's death had been something he hadn't been able to control.

Holly's behavior was something else he hadn't been able to control. He was self-centered enough to view events only as they related to or affected him. He wasn't grieved by the loss of his wife as much as infuriated by it.

With that knowledge came better understanding. Holly didn't fool herself into thinking for one minute that she was any better off staying in her father's company than before. But she came to terms with him and resolved her unspoken anger that he couldn't be the father she wanted him to be, any more than she could be the daughter he wanted.

"Why did you want to see me? What was so important that you had to send someone to track me down?"

"The business."

Of course. What other reason could there be? "I've told you before, I have no interest in the business," Holly said.

"That's not true. Your mother left her interest in the business to you, to be handed over to you on your thirtieth birthday, which is coming up in a year or two. Until that point, I as trustee have been looking after it, but I can't sell the business without reimbursing you for your shares."

"This is all news to me."

"I saw no point in telling you until it became relevant."

"And, of course, you get to decide what is and isn't relevant and when it does or doesn't become so."

"You're talking in circles."

"I'm talking about control and your overwhelming need to have it."

"I don't have control of my own company."

"Which no doubt aggravates you no end."

"I'm willing to pay you fair market value for the shares, although if you were any kind of a daughter you'd give them to me. You've never been interested in the business."

"If you'd been any kind of a father, I might have given them to you. As it is, I'll accept the offer of fair market value, which is to be donated to Inner View."

He reached for a folder on his desk and handed it to Holly. "Fine." He didn't even ask what Inner View was. "Just sign this."

Holly opened the folder and quickly read over the document inside. It was a bill of sale for her share of stock. Before signing it, she added the proviso that her representative would verify the fair market value. Byron would take care of that for her. She knew how tightly her father held on to his money and she wouldn't put it past him to try and pull a fast one on her.

"You could have mailed this to me and had me sign it," Holly told her father as she handed the document to him.

"You resented me so much, I thought you'd do something to get back at me—sell it to outsiders or something rash."

"Well, you can relax now. I'm not going to do anything to get back at you. That's more your modus operandi than mine."

"What's that supposed to mean?"

"This plot you schemed up with Rick Dunbar. It was a way to pay me back for disobeying you, wasn't it?"

"I hired the man to find you, that's all. And to do whatever it took to make you come back home."

"Whatever it took?" Even though Holly had suspected as much, actually hearing the words was like having a knife stabbed through her heart. "Like what exactly? Seducing me?"

"The guy was an idiot. Called me up and quit the job. Said he couldn't go through with it after all. He not only blew off his final five thousand, he returned the five thousand he got up front. Nice break for me."

"Wait a minute here. Back up. You said Rick called you and quit? When exactly was this?"

"I don't know... last Sunday morning, I guess."

"You guess?"

"It was definitely Sunday morning. I was on my way out to the golf course for an 11:00 a.m. tee-off time when he called."

Which meant Rick had called her father *before* he'd made love to her! He hadn't been working for her father by then. He'd quit.

"Where do you think you're going?" her father demanded.

"To find my knight in shining armor. To find Rick!"

Eleven

—

"**W**here is he?" Holly demanded once she'd finally located Rick's office. "It's imperative that I find Rick Dunbar immediately!"

"I told you, miss. I'm just the cleaning lady."

"Come on," Holly coaxed the woman with a babushka, who was pushing a vacuum cleaner. The appliance reminded Holly most vividly of the scene in her cabin when Rick freed her from the evil clutches of her own vacuum cleaner. "You must know something."

"I know he keeps a messy office and won't let me touch anything on his desk, even if it's a two-day-old donut!"

"Where's his secretary?" Holly asked.

"How should I know? I told you, the office is closed."

"Maybe I can help," Holly heard a male voice say.

She squinted against the glare of light from the open doorway. It wasn't Rick.

"Do you know where Rick is?" she demanded.

"Who are you?"

"Holly. Holly Redmond. And you are . . . ?"

"Vin. Rick's. . .associate. Yeah, I'm his associate. So why are you lookin' for Rick? Maybe I can handle your case instead. You tryin' to track down a cheatin' husband, maybe?"

"No—"

"Don't tell me. You're lookin' for someone who's missin', right?"

"Right."

"Then you've come to the right place. Dunbar and Associates specializes in findin' missing people."

"I already know that. And the sign on the door says Rick Dunbar, Private Investigator. Nothing about Dunbar and Associates."

"Rick hasn't fixed the sign yet."

"You look a little young to be an investigator. . . ." Holly noted.

"I'm older than I look. Why, I just assisted Rick in a major case up in the mountains a few days back. A very major case. I brought him valuable information and equipment."

"What kind of equipment?" Holly demanded, having a feeling that *she* was the major case up in the mountains.

"I can't tell you. It's classified information."

"What about Rick's location? Is that classified information, too?"

"I can take care of your case. . . ."

"You don't understand, Vin. This is a very personal matter. Between Rick and myself."

"Are you married?" Vin suddenly demanded.

"No. What's that got to do with anything?"

"Rick said I should always ask. . . . If ladies come looking for him, ask if they're married."

"Do a lot of ladies come looking for him?" The idea didn't please Holly.

"Only to hire him. It's pitiful." Vin heaved a sigh before quickly returning his attention to her. "Never mind. I can't talk about the boss's personal business. He'd fire me."

"Look, Vin, I'll give you two hundred dollars if you'll tell me where Rick is." She opened her wallet and waved four fifty-dollar bills at him. Time was wasting here, and she was getting desperate.

"I don't know. . . ." Vin wavered, clearly tempted by the sight of the money. "What are you plannin' on doin' to him when you find him?"

"Nothing violent, I promise you. I love him, Vin. And I think he loves me, too."

"So you're the one."

"The one what?"

"The one who's been makin' the boss impossible since he came back to town. He told me he had heart trouble, and got me real worried that I'd have to find another job. Finally I figured out that it had to be woman trouble."

"How astute of you, Vin."

"There's no need to be insultin'. . . ."

"It was a compliment, Vin."

"Oh. Well, okay then."

"So where is Rick?" Holly prompted him, waving the cash again.

"He's doin' surveillance work from his car. He's parked across the street from this address." Vin handed her a piece of paper.

"Thanks, Vin." She gave him a big hug and stuffed the money into his shirt pocket. With Rick's address in hand, she dashed out of the office.

Rick was sitting in his nondescript beige sedan, sipping cold coffee from a soggy paper cup and wondering how the hell his life had gotten so complicated. Used to be that all it took to make him happy was a thick steak and some cash in the bank. Now he couldn't even enjoy a simple cup of coffee anymore without remembering Holly and her damned herbal tea.

As he took another sip of the sludgelike black brew, he remembered the tea he'd had at Holly's cabin after they'd made love. What had made it so memorable was the tea mug, which had a frog sitting at the bottom of it. "That's because you've got to kiss a lot of frogs before you find your prince," Holly had said. "I found mine," she had added, kissing him.

Hell, he'd never claimed to be a prince, Rick noted broodingly before noticing that someone was knocking on the tinted window of the passenger door.

He must really be going off the deep end here, because the person actually looked like Holly.... Hell, it *was* Holly! Leaning over, he opened the passenger door.

She quickly scooted into the passenger seat. "Sorry to drop in on you unannounced like this, but you don't have a car phone," she said brightly. "You know, it would be a good business investment for you to have one. Or even better, maybe one of those cellular mobile phones...."

"You came here to sell me a phone?"

Holly tried not to be discouraged by his chilly tone of voice. She'd come this far, she wasn't about to back down now. "No, I came here to tell you..." Her mouth went dry and her tongue felt like it was two sizes too big. She stalled for time, hoping to be able to recoup her sputtering self-assurance. "To tell you that I took your advice and I've moved my tools from my carpetbag to a bright shiny metal toolbox. Of course, it *is* purple, but still..." Okay, this was it, she told herself. No more beating around the bush. "Umm, I also came to tell you that I love you," she blurted out. "Now I know I told you that before, but that was before I knew what I know now."

"And what do you know now?"

"That you took yourself off the case before you made love to me. That you returned all the money to my father. That you really are the man I thought you were in the beginning. Your name might be different, but the glimpses I saw of a good man—who excelled at being slightly wicked at the right time and in the right place—were the truth. You're good for me, Rick Dunbar. I have to tell you that I'm glad your name is Dunbar," she confessed, momentarily sidetracked. "It's got a much nicer ring to it than Potter. That name never suited you real well, although of course I didn't want to tell you so at the time. Even Skye commented—"

"I don't care what Skye said. I want to know what you have to say."

"Well, I have to say that you're good for me."

"How do you figure that?"

"Because your skeptical approach to life keeps me more levelheaded."

"I wouldn't say that tracking me down to a stakeout is very *levelheaded.*" To himself, Rick noted that that was what made Holly... Holly. And he loved her the way she was. Unpredictable, irreverent, passionate.

"This is a stakeout? Really? I thought it was just a routine surveillance thing. Wow. A stakeout. This is exciting. I could go for this, I think. After all, I did track you down here, so I've obviously got some investigative skills of my own..."

Smiling, Rick recalled some of the sexy investigative work she'd done on him.

"...and maybe we should work together in the future." Seeing Rick's fierce frown, Holly told him her real plans. "Actually, I am thinking of working here in Seattle in the near future. I'd like to start a project similar to the one we have at Inner View, here in the city, for underprivileged kids. Ideally I'd like to have a center here in Seattle with supplemental trips up to the mountains. It's so important to give these kids a sense of self-esteem. There's a similar program involving the arts and kids down in Los Angeles. They visit detention centers and prisons—"

"Forget it. I'm not letting you visit any prisons. Not without me there."

"Fine. You can come along. A great idea! Thanks for offering, Rick. See what I mean about us being a good team? You are good for me." Her expression changed from a teasing one to a more serious one as she continued, "You made me realize that, despite my father's domination, I really have had a fairly easy life compared to what others have had to cope with. I did have a privileged upbringing and I never had to worry growing up about where the next meal was coming from. There are plenty of people who have far greater problems, and I want to do something to help them."

"So you're going to start a new project? That seems to be a habit with you, doesn't it? To move on to something else once a project gets going. You've lived in half the states in this country in the past eight years, Holly."

"Did it ever occur to you that maybe I moved around so much because I was looking for something... for someone? You."

Holly saw the fire in Rick's eyes. She saw what was coming and she wasn't disappointed as seconds later he snared her in his arms and kissed her. It had been so long since she'd felt the magic of his lips on hers. Too long.

"Is that a proposal?" he murmured in the midst of an enticing kiss.

"Definitely not," Holly modestly denied. "I'm an old-fashioned kind of girl, didn't you know that?" She and Rick both grinned at her absurd claim. "If there's any proposing to be done, *you* can do it. However, I feel it's only fair to warn you that just because I changed the location of my tools, that doesn't mean you should expect me to change a lot. I mean, a few little things here and there, but, Rick, I'm never going to be . . . normal, I guess."

"No, you never are, thank God."

"You really don't mind?"

"No, I really don't mind. It's one of the things I love about you."

Holly's breath caught in her throat. "That's the first time you've ever said you loved me," she whispered.

"Sometimes it's hard to get a word in edgewise with you."

"You know a surefire way to shut me up."

"Mmm, that I do. But first . . . will you, Holly Redmond, take me and my tools as your husband?"

"*Yes!* Yes! Yes! Ye—"

His kiss cut off the rest of her affirmative exclamations. Their embrace quickly escalated into a sensual celebration. She rejoiced in the magic of being in his arms again. His hands cupped her ears, his fingers threading through the silky wildness of her hair as he slanted his mouth across hers with exultant passion. Holly found herself unbuttoning his shirt without even consciously knowing she was doing so. Once she had her hands on the bare warmth of his chest, she felt bonded by the connection of his flesh to hers.

Rick responded by trailing one hand down her throat to the delicate hollow above her collarbone before stealing under her blouse to finally capture the fullness of her breast. She was basking in the glow of his meticulous attention when she eventually realized where this was going. For once, she tried to be levelheaded.

"What about your case?" she huskily asked Rick. "Aren't you supposed to be working here? I don't want to interfere with your job."

"Forget my job." Rick undid her blouse and tugged her onto his lap, thankful that he'd already shoved the seat way back and tilted the steering wheel out of his way for his surveillance duty. "I've got a bad case of loving you that needs immediate attention."

"We're in a car here, Rick!" she reminded him as he lifted her full skirt out of his way and caressed the moist lush valley between her thighs.

"We're in the city, Holly. This is my turf. Trust me, I know what I'm doing."

"I can tell you do," she murmured as he tossed her underwear into the back seat and set to work on the front fastening of her bra.

"Here, scoot forward a little. Ah, yes...."

"You always did want to be in the driver's seat in our relationship," she breathlessly noted.

"Feels like we're both in the driver's seat. Hold on..." Rick adjusted the seat back to a more horizontal position.

"This is decadent."

"I know," he growled.

"I've never made love in a car before," she confessed.

"Just don't lean on the horn and we'll be fine."

"We're steaming up the windows."

"Good."

"Mmm, very good," she purred as she freed him from the confines of his jeans. "Have you got rust protection...?"

"Back pocket of my jeans," he gasped.

When she took too long, he growled a protest. "What's the problem?"

"Nothing. I was admiring the view...." she murmured provocatively.

As soon as he was fully sheathed in the latex covering, he cupped her bottom and pulled her to him. One surging thrust and she was his. Rick's growl was unintelligible, but his meaning was clear as he flexed his hips, urging her into a faster, harder rhythm.

"I can't believe... I can't believe we're really doing this!" Holly gasped.

"Believe it."

The fact that their intimate joining was camouflaged under the cover of her skirt was incredibly erotic to Holly, adding a new dimension of forbidden ecstasy and wildness to their lovemaking. "I feel...wicked."

"Not from where I'm sitting, you don't," he murmured with that naughty riverboat gambler's grin of his. "You feel... You feel incredible!"

"So do you."

"Hold on again," Rick muttered before using the electric seat adjuster.

The resultant vibration made Holly gasp with pleasure. "What was that?"

"One of my power options." Rick used the seat adjuster again.

Holly gasped again and then smiled seductively. "You know, the very first moment I saw you, I got this special hum inside.... But this...this is something else again!"

"Let's see how creative I can get, now that I've been coached by experts...."

He got to be *very* creative, indeed...making her shiver and burn at the same time. Their seductive verbal interplay was silenced by the mounting passion flaring between them. Holly closed her eyes as the inner fireworks exploded with the rush of a vibrant skyrocket. Sparklers of ecstasy radiated and shimmered their way into her very soul. Moments later, Rick reached his completion.

They stayed clasped in each other's arms until their heartbeats returned to something resembling a normal pace. Nibbling on her ear, Rick huskily whispered, "Well, this is another fine escapade you've gotten me into. Tell me, teacher, did I pass the test? Creative enough for you?''

"You're *perfect* for me," Holly replied, nestling closer. Rick couldn't argue with that.

* * * * *

SILHOUETTE
Desire

are thrilled to present
a classic twelve-book mini-series from
the ever popular, bestselling author

DIANA PALMER

TEXAN
LOVERS

Men no sane woman could resist!

The series begins with a trio of utterly
gorgeous rugged ranchers, so don't miss
Calhoun in May '96, *Justin* in June and *Tyler*
in July. And they're only the starting line-up!

One Texan Lover a month for a whole year—
it's too good to be true!

*Available from WH Smith, John Menzies, Volume One,
Forbuoys Martins, Woolworths, Tesco, Asda, Safeway and
other paperback stockists.*

SILHOUETTE

Desire

COMING NEXT MONTH

JUSTIN
Diana Palmer

Texan Lovers

Shelby Jacobs had never stopped loving dark, intense Justin Ballenger, despite the fact she'd broken their engagement. She was sure he despised her, but she knew he needed to hear the truth about the past. Shelby knew she was risking everything, but Justin was more than worth it.

PEACHY'S PROPOSAL
Carole Buck

Wedding Belles

Pam "Peachy" Keene was determined to lose her virginity, and she knew of only one man for the job—sexy Luc Devereaux. But Luc didn't want to help Peachy become 'experienced'. He *was* attracted to her, yet he knew she'd regret not waiting for the man she loved. How could he convince Peachy to change her mind?

LUCAS: THE LONER
Cindy Gerard

Sons and Lovers

Lucas Caldwell knew Kelsey Gates was trouble! The rugged cowboy sensed the big-city reporter had discovered his lifelong secret, but Kelsey claimed she wanted only one thing: *him*. Lucas was sure she was lying, but how could he turn down such a tempting offer?

COMING NEXT MONTH

WOLFE WEDDING
Joan Hohl

Big Bad Wolfe

Although wedding fever had hit his family, getting hitched was the last thing on Cameron Wolfe's mind. Sharing a cozy cabin with sexy Sandra Bradley seemed a great idea and things went well…so well that Sandra realized there was a little Wolfe on the way. She knew exactly what *she* wanted, but would the biggest, baddest Wolfe say "I do"?

COWBOY'S BRIDE
Barbara McMahon

Kalli Bonotelli had dreamed of owning a ranch with Mr Right. Now she had the ranch, all she needed was the husband…so she set her sights on handsome Trace Longford. Trouble was, he didn't want her hand—he wanted her land!

MY HOUSE OR YOURS?
Lass Small

Josephine Morris hadn't seen her ex-husband in almost four years when they were suddenly stranded in the last hotel room in Dallas—together. Chad Wilkins always had been a master in the bedroom, and now he was intent on wooing Josephine back into his life. She knew she should be strong, but how

COMING NEXT MONTH FROM
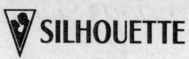 **SILHOUETTE**

Sensation
A thrilling mix of passion, adventure and drama

THE MORNING SIDE OF DAWN Justine Davis
LOVING EVANGELINE Linda Howard
IAIN ROSS'S WOMAN Emilie Richards
ANGEL AND THE BAD MAN Dallas Schulze

Intrigue
Danger, deception and desire

DARK STAR Sheryl Lynn
UNDYING LAUGHTER Kelsey Roberts
FATAL CHARM Aimée Thurlo
WHAT CHILD IS THIS? Rebecca York

Special Edition
Satisfying romances packed with emotion

JUST MARRIED Debbie Macomber
BABY ON THE DOORSTEP Cathy Gillen Thacker
MORGAN'S MARRIAGE Lindsay McKenna
CODY'S FIANCÉE Gina Ferris Wilkins
NO KIDS OR DOGS ALLOWED Jane Gentry
THE BODYGUARD & MS JONES Susan Mallery

Delicious Dishes

Would you like to win a year's supply of sophisticated and deeply emotional romances? Well, you can and they're FREE! Simply match the dish to it's country of origin and send your answers to us by 30th November 1996. The first 5 correct entries picked after the closing date will win a year's supply of Silhouette Special Editions (six books every month—worth over £160). What could be easier?

A	LASAGNE		GERMANY
B	KORMA		GREECE
C	SUSHI		FRANCE
D	BACLAVA		ENGLAND
E	PAELLA		MEXICO
F	HAGGIS		INDIA
G	SHEPHERD'S PIE		SPAIN
H	COQ AU VIN		SCOTLAND
I	SAUERKRAUT		JAPAN
J	TACOS		ITALY

Please turn over for details of how to enter

How to enter

Listed in the left hand column overleaf are the names of ten delicious dishes and in the right hand column the country of origin of each dish. All you have to do is match each dish to the correct country and place the corresponding letter in the box provided.

When you have matched all the dishes to the countries, don't forget to fill in your name and address in the space provided and pop this page into an envelope (you don't need a stamp) and post it today! Hurry—competition ends 30th November 1996.

Silhouette Delicious Dishes
FREEPOST
Croydon
Surrey
CR9 3WZ

Are you a Reader Service Subscriber?   Yes ❑   No ❑

Ms/Mrs/Miss/Mr _____

Address _____

_____

_____ Postcode _____

One application per household.

You may be mailed with other offers from other reputable companies as a result of this application. If you would prefer not to receive such offers, please tick box. ❑

C196
E